W0115370

By Andi Lee

ANIMAL LARK
Mischief Maker

Published by Dreamspinner Press
www.dreamspinnerpress.com

# mischief MAKER

## ANDI LEE

DREAMSPINNER PRESS

Published by

DREAMSPINNER PRESS

5032 Capital Circle SW, Suite 2, PMB# 279, Tallahassee, FL 32305-7886 USA
www.dreamspinnerpress.com

This is a work of fiction. Names, characters, places, and incidents either are the product of author imagination or are used fictitiously, and any resemblance to actual persons, living or dead, business establishments, events, or locales is entirely coincidental.

Mischief Maker
© 2019 Andi Lee

Cover Art
© 2019 Reece Notley
reece@vitaenoir.com
Cover content is for illustrative purposes only and any person depicted on the cover is a model.

All rights reserved. This book is licensed to the original purchaser only. Duplication or distribution via any means is illegal and a violation of international copyright law, subject to criminal prosecution and upon conviction, fines, and/or imprisonment. Any eBook format cannot be legally loaned or given to others. No part of this book may be reproduced or transmitted in any form or by any means, electronic or mechanical, including photocopying, recording, or by any information storage and retrieval system, without the written permission of the Publisher, except where permitted by law. To request permission and all other inquiries, contact Dreamspinner Press, 5032 Capital Circle SW, Suite 2, PMB# 279, Tallahassee, FL 32305-7886, USA, or www.dreamspinnerpress.com.

Trade Paperback ISBN: 978-1-64405-422-2
Digital ISBN: 978-1-64405-421-5
Library of Congress Control Number: 2019932539
Trade Paperback published August 2019
v. 1.0

Printed in the United States of America
∞
This paper meets the requirements of
ANSI/NISO Z39.48-1992 (Permanence of Paper).

To Jean-Claude and Asher, the best of rats,
and to The Five, the best of friends.
Also to my parents for always believing in me.

# Acknowledgements

FIRSTLY TO TA Moore, who convinced me that people would read a story about two men falling in love at a rat show. I'm not sure this would ever have been more than an idea without her not-so-gentle prodding! To Justine, who took me bat detecting many years ago and also helped me flesh out Jamie's career. To the organisers of the UKMeet for putting together such an amazing event with so many opportunities. I don't think I'd be here without it. And finally a huge thank-you to everyone at Dreamspinner for being so welcoming and taking a chance on me and my rat-loving boys.

# Chapter One

*A GROUP of Rats is Called a Mischief*
  Zombie Brum City
  *L_ofa_Ride*
  223K Views. 8 days ago
  Liam barely remembered a time when his vlog wasn't the most important thing in his life. As friends settled down into nine-to-five jobs and found partners, his life became less ordinary—just the way he liked it. If he ever felt a twinge of dissatisfaction, he would check how many new subscribers he had and scroll through his comments. His life was fun.

  He used his phone camera to check his appearance. His hair was too perfect, so he ruffled it with one hand until it fell into his eyes. When he deemed it tousled enough, he nodded, switched over to video mode, and pressed play.

  "Two words," he said in the conspiring tone he used to draw his viewers in and create intimacy. "*Escape Room.*"

  His vlogging camera was a Panasonic Lumix, but when he was out and about, he liked the effect he got when he edited the lower spec on his phone into footage from the Lumix. It gave it a fake-reporter vibe.

  "In hindsight I shouldn't have taken a hookup I met on Quirky Gay Guys to Zombie Brum City." He winked. "I know what you're all saying—he's had worse dates. I have indeed had worse dates, but never have I ever let my date get eaten by zombies." He exaggerated each movement and bit at his lips, knowing his viewers would eat it up. It was a look he'd practiced in the mirror, so he knew it was good.

  Liam's mom called him flighty, and his dad said he was blessed with the pretty gene and would settle down eventually. Liam didn't know about that. He'd never found a man he wanted for more than one night. And it wasn't like he hadn't tried.

Zombie Brum City was an escape room in Digbeth, just ten minutes from Birmingham City centre. Digbeth had been in development since the Bullring opened years earlier, but it was still mostly full of abandoned factories and derelict buildings. The warehouse was easy to overlook from the road. It wasn't any different from the other buildings—tall, red bricked, with broken windows held together by nothing more than dirt and age. The Zombie Brum City sign was rusted and had a fake bullet hole and a bloody handprint—not much different at all.

Liam sat on the toilet in a cubicle. It wasn't an actual escape room, just an average toilet painted to look like zombies were pulling open the doors and their decaying fingers had left bloody marks along the edge. It was a little off-putting.

There was no one else in there, but he whispered anyway. "It turns out they frown upon people getting busy in their rooms. And my date didn't enjoy being sacrificed to the zombies. But hey, in a zombie apocalypse, it's every man for himself. Wait… shit, did you hear that?" He hadn't heard anything, but he gave the camera a shake. "Shit."

He unlocked the door, peered around, and tiptoed out into the corridor.

"All clear. I should try to get out of here."

To be fair, the night wasn't all a lie. He *had* found his date on an app called Quirky Gay Guys, he *did* get caught getting a blow job, and he *did* sacrifice his date to the zombie gods. And he was almost home free when he rounded the corner and saw his date—he should try to remember his name—at the other end of the room.

"Oi," he shouted as he strode toward Liam, eyes blazing.

"Oh shit," Liam said into his phone, unable to contain his excitement. It was too good. He ran toward the doors, camera pointing at his feet. Then he crashed into two guys just outside. Flailing in an attempt to regain his balance, he grabbed on to the nearest person.

The man tried to keep them both upright, but they teetered sideways, arms and legs tangling as they crashed to the ground. Liam couldn't stop the fall, but he was able to twist at the last minute so he landed underneath.

His head hit the gravel, which made his eyes water, and he had less than a second before the stranger landed on top of him and pushed the air from his lungs with an *oof.* The man's curly brown hair ended up in his mouth, and his knee was dangerously close to Liam's balls as he scrambled on top of Liam, trying to get up.

He let out a stream of curses as he got to his feet, his friend steadying him. "Are you okay, darling?" the friend asked.

Liam froze, still on the ground, but not because he was hurt.

"I'm fine," the brunet said as he patted dirt off his clothes. He glared down at Liam. "You should watch where you're going."

Liam managed to suck in air through smiling lips and slowly sat up. "Sorry. It was an emergency." He looked around to see if he was still being chased.

The back of his head throbbed, and he gingerly pressed it with his fingers to see if he was bleeding.

"He's hurt." The other guy bent down toward him and moved his hand away so he could look. He parted Liam's hair and felt around the knot that was forming there.

"Serves himself right." The man he'd run into folded his arms and looked out into the traffic across the carpark. Liam watched him with interest. He found his grumpiness endearing, and the grumpier he appeared, the more amused Liam became. Perhaps he'd hit his head harder than he originally thought.

"You're not bleeding, and your brain isn't leaking from your ears, darling. Any double vision?"

Liam shook his head but then wished he hadn't. "Are you a doctor?" There was something in the way he touched Liam's head that showed more knowledge than the average person.

The man gave a soft laugh and stood up. "You could say that. I'm a vet." He held out his hand to Liam and pulled him up. The other guy was still looking anywhere but at them.

"Well, thanks for the checkup." Liam looked to the other man and said, "I really am sorry. I hope I didn't hurt you."

He gave a grunt, looked back for a second, and stormed off through the doors. Liam watched him, and when his gaze flickered to the guy's tight arse, he smiled. Mr Grumpy was cute. A coil of affection tightened in his belly, and laughter bubbled from his lips as he remembered their tangled limbs and the look of annoyance that had crossed his face.

"Thanks again," he said.

The vet gave him a salute and then said, "No problem. I had to make sure you weren't too hurt." He nodded toward the door, and Liam looked up, eyes connecting with Mr Grumpy through the glass. He bit back a smiled. "Don't worry about him, he's in a bit of a mood. Ta-ra a bit." Then he turned around to go inside.


JAMIE GROUND his teeth together and stood impatiently in the reception, waiting for Dane. The man behind the counter was talking animatedly to another guy, and they both ignored him, which suited Jamie just fine. He stepped toward a poster on the opposite wall and pretended to read it, but he couldn't take in the information. He fished out his mobile from his pocket. Nothing from Paul, not a text or a missed call. Nothing.

This was meant to be a fun night out, something different than going to the pub and getting drunk like usual, but it had all gone to shit. It hurt that it was his boyfriend and best friend who had blown him off. If it was a night at the village, they'd be the first there. He tried to push down the pain and annoyance and stared toward the door. At least Dane was there—even if he was hitting on that dickhead. The glow of a streetlamp showed them talking and laughing, and the annoyance he'd tried to swallow came back up again.

Jamie rolled his eyes. Typical Dane, hitting on any pretty boy he found. He'd be fighting zombies alone at this rate. He glared through the glass, and as if he could feel the daggers he was shooting his way, the stranger looked up, and their eyes connected. A crackle of something—awareness, anger, Jamie wasn't sure—shot through him, and he had to drag his eyes away.

He needed to get a grip. He wasn't usually so highly strung, but Paul had been acting strange for a while, and he didn't know what to do about it. The door slid open, and Dane stepped over the threshold. Jamie sighed in relief. *Finally*.

"Done flirting?" Jamie asked. He sounded childish to his own ears, but he couldn't stop the words falling from his mouth.

Dane laughed and flung an arm around his shoulders, which made it hard for him to stay mad. "You are in such a mood tonight, darling. I was just making sure he wasn't concussed."

"What about me? I'm the one he crashed into." Jamie looked down at his jeans that still had dirt and gravel clinging to the knees. Dane bent down and made a show of brushing the dirt off until Jamie's lips twitched in an attempt at a smile and he stepped back.

"Happy now? You need to lighten up. It's not every day a gorgeous hot stranger ploughs into you." Dane wiggled his eyebrows and licked his lips.

"You are disgusting." Jamie pushed him away playfully. "I didn't notice what he looked like. I was too busy trying not to break a leg, thank you very much. We are going to be so late for our session."

"No need to be pissy with me. I'm not the one you're mad at, darling. I'm here, aren't I? I swapped night shifts at the practice, so I'm going to be working double weekends for you."

Jamie winced, realising what a selfish bastard he was being. He sometimes forgot not everyone had the luxury of picking their hours like he did. Dane swapping shifts meant he wouldn't be able to go out partying on the weekend because he'd have to stay at the veterinary surgery to look after the animals staying overnight.

"I'm sorry, I appreciate it, I really do. I'm glad you're here." He forced a large smile over his face, though he was sure Dane didn't buy it. "Shall we see if we can survive a horde of zombies?"

Dane tipped back his head and laughed. "Darling, I thought you'd never ask." Jamie held out his arm, and Dane linked his with Jamie's as they walked over to the two men at the reception desk and interrupted their conversation.

# Chapter Two

*Mr Liam Donnelly,*
*Miss Alison Thorn and Mr Frank Hamilton request*
*the pleasure of your company at their marriage.*

Liam threw his jacket over the back of the sofa and flipped the invitation in his hands. No plus-one? That was odd. Maybe it was a mistake. He only spoke to his cousin last week, and nothing was mentioned then.

He needed a cuppa. He'd spent the whole day giving back-to-back driving lessons, and he was knackered. He filled the kettle, and while he waited for it to boil, he looked in on Mabel.

"Hey, girl, did you have a good day?" He shook a tin of treats and grinned when she twitched her nose at him and launched herself at the bars. Mabel was a tart for a yoghurt drop. She reached out to him with one humanlike paw, and he placed a treat in it. Then she ran off and hid it in her bed.

He fell in love with Mabel at a pet shop a few weeks ago when he went to buy a dog to show his family and friends he could be responsible. Apparently puppies in pet shop windows were a myth, but he saw hamsters, rabbits, and rats. Mabel was in the adoption section all alone, and she'd looked at him with her black eyes. It was love.

Once she'd eaten her treat, she came back out and demanded cuddles. He opened the door, and she ran up his arm to his shoulder. "Who's a good girl? Now I wonder what the hell Frank is playing at? Shall we ask Auntie Bethan if she knows what's going on?"

Mabel settled down. He grabbed his phone and opened FaceTime, hoping Beth would answer. She answered quickly, and he could tell she was in her dorm room at uni. There were other people with her, so she stood quickly and put her hand up so he'd wait before speaking.

*What's up, fat face?* She signed at him using BSL. He rolled his eyes and gave her the middle finger. Both Beth and their mother were profoundly deaf, and he'd learned British Sign Language from birth, so it was second nature to him. The invention of Skype and FaceTime meant it was so much easier for them to stay in touch now she was away at uni. They were able to do more than just text each other, which was very handy, especially when he had a very important question.

*Did you get an invitation from Frank and Alice?*

She nodded. *They sent it to Mom and Dad's.*

*Did you get a plus-one?* Liam said.

*I did. I'm taking my boyfriend. Why?*

Liam cursed out loud. How could they do that? Beth didn't deserve a plus-one. She was practically a child. *Frank didn't give me a plus-one.*

Beth grinned and laughed. It was the only sound she made. He waited impatiently for her to look at him again, and he gave her two fingers, which just made her laugh harder. His family sucked. *You suck,* he signed, then pressed End.

"Shall we go around to Frank and Alice's and have it out?" he asked Mabel. She ground her teeth happily, and he took that as a yes. "By *us* I mean me. You can have another treat, though."

FRANK AND Alice had been living together for eight years, and they owned a nice semidetached house in Sutton Coldfield, not too far from Lockstone, where Liam and the rest of Frank's family lived.

Liam drummed his fingers against the sides of his thighs as he waited at the door. What was taking so long? Frank finally answered with a smile that quickly dropped when he realised it was Liam.

"Oh. Hi. I see you got the invitation?"

Liam rolled his eyes, pushed past him, and marched straight to the kitchen to make himself a cup of coffee and eat all the good biscuits. Tea wouldn't cut it this time.

"What the hell, Frankie?" He purposefully used the childhood nickname to rub in their shared history.

Frank was a tall, bulky guy who played rugby and had one cauliflower ear that he hid beneath his shaggy mop of hair. He towered over Liam, who wasn't short by any means, but he'd never been intimidated by the huge lump, and he wasn't going to start now.

"You gave my sister a plus-one, but not me?"

"I told Alice you'd notice that."

"I don't get it. Why did Beth get a plus-one and I didn't?"

"It's because we don't trust you not to use our wedding in your vlog, bab. You're the best man—you need to be respectful," Alice said, and he jumped as she walked into the kitchen behind him. She pressed a kiss to his cheek to show she wasn't mad.

He didn't think it was wise to tell her he didn't need to have a plus-one to hook up at their wedding. In fact, a date might rein him in.

"I wouldn't do that to you guys." Although it would have gotten great views.

Frank gave him an affectionate shove over the table and stole a custard cream. "Didn't you do that at Uncle Kev's wedding last year? I'm sure that's why they emigrated to America. He's still having flashbacks of you banging the waiter behind the bins."

Liam groaned. He was never going to live that down. "What groom takes out his own rubbish?"

"The kind trying to get away from his ball and chain," Frank said, laughing.

"Don't be upset, lovely." Everyone was *lovely* or *bab* to Alice. "We're proud your vlog thing is successful. We're even prouder that your driving business is getting off the ground. But I won't have *my wedding*"—she said "my wedding" as though it had nothing to do with Frank—"as the butt of one of your YouTube videos. Okay?"

She took the packet of biscuits, folded the edges closed, and put them back in the cupboard. Liam glared at the back of her head. He hadn't finished with those. "I wouldn't even contemplate using your wedding in one of my videos." He was a bit hurt they'd even thought that.

"Maybe not, but what kind of plus-one would you be bringing, and would we want them at our wedding, eating our very expensive food or in our photos?" Frank looked at Alice with lovesick puppy-dog eyes that made Liam want to vomit. "Let's be honest, Liam. They'd be in our life much longer than they'd be in yours."

Liam ground his teeth, desperately wanting to argue but unable to because it was true. Bloody hell. "What about if I took Selena?" Selena was his best friend, and she could be his fake date for the day.

Alice rolled her eyes as she pottered around the kitchen, tidying up the coffee he'd left out. "Selena and Dawn are already invited. What? Don't you think your friends talk to each other when you're not around? The world doesn't revolve around you, you know."

"Great. Everyone can take someone apart from me. I'll be the loner sitting in the corner. I'll be Baby, only I won't have Patrick Swayze to come rescue me so we can dance 'Y.M.C.A.' together."

"Pretty sure that's not how *Dirty Dancing* ended," Frank said, eyes sparkling with humour, more resolved. Liam hated that look.

Frank glanced over his head as though getting permission. Liam frowned and turned around to see what Alice was up to, but she just stood next to the fridge writing small notes on the to-do list stuck to the door.

"Look," Frank said. Liam turned back around. "If you start seeing someone seriously—and by serious, I mean no one-night stands, no hookups, no fuck buddies. If you can prove to me—" Alice coughed. "—prove to *us* that you are in a serious, committed relationship, then we might change our minds."

"What am I, a kid?" Liam scowled. He was sure they'd given no one else an ultimatum.

"Well, if you don't want a plus-one…."

It's not that he was bothered about taking anyone to their wedding, but it was the principle of the thing. He was going to earn that plus-one, and his date would be in every bloody one of their photos. "No, I do. I'll do it."

"It's not a game," Alice warned him.

"You're right. Your wedding isn't a game." It was all in the wording. So he couldn't film at their wedding, but anything before and after was fair.

# Chapter Three

THE GREAT Rat-Show Date Hunt
*L_ofa_Ride*
578K Views. 4 days ago

Liam decided to go to the National Fancy Rat Show after a subscriber suggested he would find the man of his dreams there. He highly doubted it, but if he could find someone he could stand to be around long enough to keep Frank and Alice happy, then it would be enough.

The rat show was in one of huge halls at the Staffordshire County Showground. It was a sprawling place nestled between rolling hills and lush green trees. Signs pointed the way, but it was self-explanatory—he just followed the people with the rats.

The show was already heaving when he got there, and with Mabel on his shoulder, he went to investigate. He imagined rats doing tricks, jumping through hoops, and dancing like the dogs on *Britain's Got Talent*. He was disappointed when all the show rats had to do was sit in a tank and look pretty.

Where was the talent in that?

He moved away from the show rats toward the stalls around the outside of the room where they sold rat-related items. One woman was drawing miniature rat portraits, and another made rat ornaments, while others sold handmade rat treats. One stall in particular stood out with its brightly coloured squares of fabric. He spotted something with *Ghostbusters* on it and picked it up, realising it was a hammock. The fleece was soft against his hand, and he could picture it hanging in Mabel's cage. As if she knew what he was thinking, Mabel's nose twitched and she poked her head from out of his hair.

"Like it, do you?" He turned his face toward her and rubbed his cheek against her fur.

"You a *Ghostbusters* fan?" the lady behind the stall said with a smile. On her T-shirt she had a sticker of a rat with a speech bubble saying *Jan.*

"Who doesn't love *Ghostbusters*? These hammocks are amazing." He looked at some of her others, each of them in funky material with bright fleece lining. He felt like a rat-father failure right then, because Mabel's hammocks were made from cheap pillowcases he'd gotten from Wilkos and hacked into something resembling a square.

"I made a few others in the same fabric, if you wanted matching." She showed him a large hammock and a pouch that went around his neck so rats could feel safe outside the cage. Mabel was comfortable riding his shoulders, but she might like to chill in one of those.

"Your rat is a sweetie. Can I hold her while you browse? I didn't bring my boys. Too much other stuff in the car." She looked at Mabel longingly, and Liam handed her over, hating to see her so sad. "Oh, she is so sweet," Jan said.

"She really is. I adopted her a few months ago, and she's really come out of her shell now. I'm thinking of getting her some friends. I read that they like company." He'd watched so many rat YouTube videos it made him want to start a dedicated channel just for Mabel.

"That's a great idea. It's called GMR, you know."

Liam blinked and frowned. Had he heard her correctly? There was quite a bit of background noise. "GMR?" What was that? Had he caught some rat-related disease? Did he have the plague?

She nodded and smiled as though she were sharing a secret with him. "Get. More. Rats. It's how we all start. One rat, then three, then five, then twenty. Once you start, you can't stop." She laughed, and he grinned along with her in relief.

"How much for these three?" Mabel needed *Ghostbuster* hammocks in her life.

"Thirty-five pounds for the set. I made them all by hand. And you're right—they're much happier with rat friends. You should talk to some of the breeders here. Jamie's over there. His rats are beautiful. I taught him everything I know. Mind you, he's got a waiting list a mile long." She absently sniffed Mabel's belly. It was only a little strange to see, but Mabel was definitely lapping up the attention, so he didn't try to rescue her just yet.

"Are you a breeder too?" Liam asked as he handed over money and she reluctantly handed Mabel back.

"I am, but I'm having a bit of a break at the moment because my husband and I will be moving house soon. It'll be hard enough with eighteen rats, let alone rat kittens."

She put the hammocks into a bag for him, but Liam put the pouch around his neck and held it up for Mabel to investigate. She sniffed at it, then gingerly stepped inside. He let it hang around his neck, and she nestled down, eyes boggling.

"I think she likes it," he said. He liked it too. He didn't have to worry about her slipping off his shoulder.

Jan nodded. "A definite success. You have a good time at the show, you hear? And don't be a stranger in the community."

He said his goodbyes and made his way around the show. A cute guy with short brown hair and green eyes smiled at him from over the show tanks. Liam smiled back, and a flicker of interest stirred. He'd almost forgotten why he'd come to the show in the first place. The guy made his way over to Liam, hips swaying as he dodged around the people in his way.

"Hi, I'm Rowan. It's crazy here, isn't it? It's my first time at a show," he said.

It couldn't be this easy. Liam thought the chances of finding a compatible gay man were slim to none, so to have a guy hit on him almost straightaway was a bit of an ego booster.

"Liam. Tell me about it. It's my first time too. It's great. Did you see how huge that rat is over there?" Liam pointed behind him, but all he could see now were people. "Did you bring any rats with you?"

Rowan shook his head and gave a little laugh. "No, I don't have any rats. I did come to find something here, though."

Liam nodded in understanding. "Are you getting rat kittens from some of the breeders here? I heard Jamie is brilliant."

Rowan gave a noncommittal answer. "He's good, yes. It's so packed in here. Do you want to go get a coffee?" He sounded so eager.

Liam hadn't finished browsing yet, and he had Mabel with him. And there was something about Rowan that didn't sit right with him—probably that he hadn't commented on how amazing Mabel was. But Rowan was cute, and he would look good in Alice's photos.

He smiled at the thought, and Rowan's face lit up. But just as he was about to agree to that coffee, Liam saw something from the corner of his eye—a glimpse of familiar curly hair and the low rumbling of a pissed-off voice.

No. It couldn't be. Surely. Liam smiled and stepped forward. He stared blatantly at the back of his curly hair, and excitement ran through his body. It took him too long to realise that Mr Grumpy wasn't alone. Not only was he not alone, there was a heated exchange of words going on. Liam knew it was wrong, but he tried to listen anyway.

He couldn't see Mr Grumpy's lips move, but he could read his companion's. He'd always been told never to use his superpowers for evil, but he had a feeling this was an exception.

"Oh. That's Jamie," Rowan said.

The world worked in mysterious ways. It must be the same Jamie who Jan had spoken about. He knew that unmistakable hair, had felt that body tangle with his. He stepped around Rowan, all interest lost. "Actually I need to speak with him. Catch you later."

Even though he only caught one side of the conversation, he guessed what their stifled argument was about. And if he guessed right, then Mr Grumpy was having a bad time.

Interest piqued, Liam tried not to be too excited that Mr Grumpy, aka Jamie the Rat Breeder, was in the process of splitting up from his boyfriend.

That could work very well in his favour. Not even the smidgen of guilt he felt was enough to stop him going over. He had a perfectly good shoulder, and Jamie might be in need of it.

Before he analysed it too much, he stepped behind Jamie and glared at the ex-boyfriend.

The ex-boyfriend's eyes widened, and as Jamie took a step backwards, Liam cupped Jamie's shoulders and turned him around, making him gasp. The can of Diet Coke in his hand wobbled dangerously.

"Hello again." He didn't know what he was going to say until he said it. "I hear you could have my babies." Liam winked, and Jamie's can of Diet Coke flew from his hand and sprayed Liam's blue jeans. It wasn't exactly how he expected the conversation to go, but it was a good icebreaker.

Jamie gave a strangled gasp, body tensing as he stepped back. "You. Shit, fuck," he said as his eyes followed the stain of Diet Coke. He blushed, lips pursed.

"I'm glad you remember me. After all, I want to be the father to some of your fur children." Once the thought took root, he couldn't stop playing with it.

Jamie didn't laugh. He just made another noise in the back of his throat, but at least he didn't sound pissed off anymore.

The ex watched them, looking puzzled and probably annoyed at being interrupted.

The silence between the three of them was thick, but Liam didn't feel awkward. He was going to get Jamie out of a shitty situation, and it felt good knowing he could do that.

"You ready to go for that coffee so we can catch up?" Liam was insinuating that he knew Jamie more than he did, but it was fun to watch the different expressions run over the boyfriend's face. He wasn't going to be the one who walked away first.

"Yeah… I mean yes. Of course. Okay," Jamie rambled. Liam laughed low in his chest, slipped an arm around Jamie's shoulders, tucked him in tight, and walked him away.

"We weren't finished," the ex shouted after them. He was a piece of work. Who split up with someone in public? Liam resisted the urge to turn around and give him the finger.

There was nowhere quiet for them to go, nowhere Jamie could compose himself, so Liam steered him outside, toward his car, and motioned him to get in.

"Don't worry. I'm not going to drive off with you and take you to the woods." But maybe to a wedding….

Jamie slid into the passenger side with a sad laugh. "I'm actually quite good in the woods." He took a deep breath, leaned back against the headrest, and closed his eyes.

Liam took the time to study him while his eyes were closed. He was leaner than Liam, but solid, with strong arms and wild brown hair that suggested he wasn't the type to bother with much styling.

When his eyes opened again, he looked mad. "What the fuck did you do that in there for?" Mr Grumpy was back. Good, he liked Mr Grumpy.

Liam shrugged in explanation. "I wanted to apologise to you again for crashing into you. And I don't like to see a damsel in distress." He knew that would annoy him.

Jamie scowled at him and dragged his hand through his hair. "I am not a damsel."

Liam's lips fought not to curl. Jamie's anger shouldn't taste so sweet.

JAMIE COULD not believe he was in a stranger's car, trying not to cry. And not only that, the stranger just happened to be the arsehole who ran into him the other night outside the escape room.

Could his day get any more shitty? A bubble of hysteria escaped his lips. Better that than sobs, he guessed.

The arsehole shrugged. "Sorry. Seemed like you needed rescuing."

"I didn't need rescuing," he said, anger sharpening his tone. He was a grown man. He could look after himself, even when his boyfriend decided to split up with him after living together for only two months. Was he really that bad to be around?

"I've not locked the doors. You can leave if you want." He took the rat out of her pouch and placed her back in her plastic carrier.

A twinge of guilt made Jamie's stomach clench. *Fuck.* "I left my rats unattended." He'd forgotten all about them. Wouldn't Paul just love that?

Despite Jamie's less-than-inviting attitude, his would-be saviour looked up from his rat, concern furrowing his brow. "Want me to nip in and get them?"

Jamie shook his head. With his luck, the guy would come back with two completely different rats. "I'll just text a friend to look after them." He fired off a text and noticed the missed calls on his phone.

*Tommy*. His best friend. *Ex*-best friend. Jamie swallowed, and something must have shown on his face, because the stranger touched his shoulder. Jamie flinched. He couldn't take kindness right then. Kindness would break him. The man dropped his hand, and Jamie could breathe.

Or so he thought. He coughed, trying to dislodge the lump at the back of his throat. "I don't even know who the hell you are… apart from the guy who gave me two skinned knees." The attempt at a joke fell flat when neither of them laughed.

"My name's Liam. I'd say it's a pleasure to meet you, but I doubt you feel the same."

That was true. First Liam ran into him when he'd been so angry that Paul and Tommy blew them off at the escape room. Then he had to witness the most humiliating event of his life—surpassing getting his head flushed down the toilet in high school while on the hunt for the elusive blue goldfish.

"I'm Jamie." There. That was a good attempt at conversation. He'd give himself a pat on the back if he didn't think he would crack from the pressure.

Liam grinned. "I know. Jamie the Rat Breeder." He said it as though it were a title or some special ability. If only.

Jamie attempted to give him a small smile, but it twisted, and the tears he thought he'd kept at bay so well finally fell down his cheeks. Damn traitorous body.

"It's okay, buddy. Let it out. He's a bastard for dumping you, especially in the middle of a crowded room."

Jamie leaned forward in the passenger seat. The sickeningly sweet smell of Little Trees air freshener made his stomach lurch. He couldn't look at Liam right then.

Throwing up was not an option. Humiliation twisted with the pain until he thought he would choke on it, and he shouldn't be crying in some stranger's car, but he couldn't make himself leave either. There was something strangely… comforting about crying in front of a stranger rather than friends.

"How did you know he was breaking up with me?" Jamie looked at Liam, vision blurry with tears. He was not a crier. Why was he doing it now?

Liam shrugged, and the leather of his jacket creaked. "I can lip-read."

Great. He'd heard Paul admit to leaving him for none other than Jamie's best friend. "That's a good skill to have." All the more to humiliate him with.

Today was meant to be a good day for him. He'd been asked to help judge the rat show for the first time. It made him feel he'd made it as a rat breeder, and all he wanted was his boyfriend there to support him. He should have known it would go wrong. Paul hated rats, but Jamie had pushed and badgered, laying on the guilt after Paul stood him up at the zombie escape room.

"I have to go back in there. I'm judging the rat show." The last thing he wanted was to head back into that hall and put on a fake smile, but he was *not* going to let Paul take that away from him.

He sat back up, feeling stronger, outwardly at least. Then he blinked the tears away and took a deep, calming breath.

"You're judging? That is so cool." Liam truly sounded excited. Why couldn't Paul sound like that? "I'll come with you, if you don't mind. After all, I do still want to talk to you about buying rats."

Jamie was surprised Liam brought that up; he'd been sure it was just a line. He looked out the window and watched people mill about the car park. When Paul stepped out of the doorway, he tensed.

A sharp pain shot through his chest as he took in his perfectly styled hair, the trendy jeans, and black suspenders over a light-blue shirt. He was so confident in his style, and Jamie had loved that about him. Paul walked across the car park as though he hadn't just broken Jamie's heart.

His eyes burned again, and Jamie bit the inside of his cheek to distract himself with the pain.

"I can thump him, if that would make you feel better," Liam said a little too eagerly.

Jamie gave a twist of the lips—not quite a smile, but he wasn't crying either. "Maybe later. I better get back in there."

Liam stuck by his side as they reentered the hall. The hairs on the back of Jamie's neck stood on end as he ignored the questioning looks from the other judges. He'd arrived that morning with one man, and now he was there with another. It must have looked odd, but he didn't have the energy to worry about it.

He found Jan behind her hammock stall. She smiled at him, and then her eyes widened and her mouth dropped when she saw Liam. "I see you found Jamie, then."

Jamie looked between the two of them, confused. "You were looking for me?"

"I was looking for Jamie the Amazing Rat Breeder. I had no clue it was you. Small world, isn't it?"

"I didn't realise you knew each other." Jan practically vibrated, wanting all the details. She would be insufferable until she extracted them all.

"We don't know each other," Jamie said in a clipped tone.

"Or we didn't until I crashed into him—literally—last week." Liam grinned and bumped his shoulder against Jamie's.

Jamie frowned at him. They didn't know each other enough to be that familiar. He took a step sideways, putting more space between them.

Jan's eyes widened. "Oh, you're the *dickhead* who gave him skinned knees?" She fanned herself with a paper bag. "I know plenty of guys who would love to get skinned knees from him."

Jamie felt his cheeks burn. "Jan!" He glanced at Liam, who was grinning from ear to ear and looked much too happy with himself. He'd probably been told his whole life how gorgeous he was.

"What?" Jan said. "It's true. And a few girls too, eh? Now tell me why your eyes are red and puffy. Has Paul left already? I thought he was staying to watch you judge."

Jamie swallowed the sudden lump in his throat. He'd gone at least three whole minutes without thinking about Paul. His eyes burned with unshed tears, and he took a deep breath to compose himself. "Paul and I are no longer an item." He could tell she was going to ask more, but he couldn't answer her questions—not now, not when he was judging a rat show in less than twenty minutes. "I'll fill you in on everything later."

"All right, dear. Why don't you both sit down here for a bit. You've got time for a cup of tea before you judge. I'll grab you both one. You can show Liam photos of your rat kittens." She was gone before he could say he didn't want a cup of tea. *Oh well.* He squeezed between the stalls and sat down. Liam sat next to him, waiting.

"Would you like to see photos? I have some on my phone." He said it all a little rushed, not smooth at all. Would he always be a mess in front of this guy?

"Definitely."

Jamie pulled his phone out of his jean pocket, and before he could hand it over, Liam got out of his chair and knelt next to him, putting an arm across the back of his chair to keep his balance.

"They're here somewhere…," Jamie mumbled. He scrolled through his photos, and Liam knelt closer, looking at photos even though he hadn't got to the rats yet.

Where were they? He scrolled frantically. The last handful he'd taken were of him and Paul, their arms around each other, looking happy. Jamie knew it was a lie now. There was another one of him and Tommy, and that was like a punch to the stomach. He sucked in a breath and scrolled fast, but he relaxed as he came to a few of the rats and tilted the phone toward Liam.

"These are some of my bucks. That's Poe and Wilde. That's one of my does, Agatha. I'm planning on breeding her soon."

"Could I get any of your kittens? They are so sweet." He leaned in closer to Jamie, his leather jacket creaking as it pressed against his arm.

Jamie let out a shaky breath. Was that some kind of line? What was he playing at? He wished he knew, but his head was all over the place, and he couldn't decide if Liam was genuine or not.

"I've got waiting lists. You probably wouldn't get any from my next few litters." Maybe that would put him off.

"That's okay. We'll wait. Won't we, Mabel?" He tutted at the little carrier she was now in. She sniffed at the holes in the top, then went back to eating her cucumber slice.

"These are kittens from my last litter."

Liam leaned even closer to peer at the photo, hand on Jamie's shoulder to keep his balance. "So cute." Jamie glanced at him, but his face was too close, so he looked back at the phone and slid it onto the desk.

Liam sat back in his own chair as Jan came back with two cups of tea. "Did he manage to show you his photos? I wasn't even sure he knew how. Stupid boy only got a smartphone a few months ago, and he only got it so he could take photos of the rats and put them on his new Facebook group. He's utterly useless with it."

Jamie rolled his eyes and smiled, knowing she was trying to keep his spirits up and his mind distracted. "I'm not that bad. I'm just not into social media. It's good helping me stay in contact with the rat community, but that's about it."

Liam laughed and shook his head. Jamie raised his eyebrow in question. "We are complete opposites in that regard. I live for social media."

# Chapter Four

JAMIE PICKED at the grain in the table and scraped the varnish away with his blunt nail. He'd avoided going out for weeks, but finally Dane and Markus had not taken no for an answer. It was gig night, after all.

They sat on the opposite side of the booth, making him feel more like a third wheel than he ever had before, which was stupid because they weren't even a couple.

"I'll kill him, darling," Dane said, voice hard. Jamie glanced up, hating to see the compassion in his eyes.

God, he was pathetic. Jamie had been so happy to be in a relationship that he'd looked over the cracks when they started to form.

"I'll kill them both." Markus took a gulp of his lager and slammed it a bit too hard on the table. They both seemed genuinely shocked about Tommy and Paul.

Jamie had a nasty thought that they might have known what was going on behind his back, but their reactions were too genuine to be faked.

"How could they?" Dane was as surprised as he was. "I know Paul was a bit of a one before you got together, but I thought he'd finally calmed down."

Jamie grunted and took a sip of his beer. He'd always loved being the one who tamed Wild Paul Harrison, but that made him feel more of a fool than usual right then. "Well, Tommy is welcome to him." His voice caught, and he took another sip, hoping to blame it on the liquid.

"This is why I always say that friends shouldn't get together. What happens when the relationship falls apart? The other friends are stuck in the middle," Markus said.

Jamie frowned and bit back his annoyance. "Yes, because the breakdown of my relationship is all about you." Markus had the decency to look apologetic. "Don't worry, I won't ask you to choose. I'm a big boy." He wished he weren't. He wanted nothing more than to demand their mutual friends pick a side, preferably his side, and cast Paul and Tommy out into the cold. But he wasn't that much of a bastard, more's the pity.

"A little birdy told me there was a handsome bloke there to help you through it, though." Dane raised an eyebrow. "Do tell."

Bloody Jan. He didn't want to talk about Liam.

"There's nothing to tell. It's not like I'll be seeing him again." Not anytime soon, anyway.

Speak of the devil. His phone decided to vibrate in his pocket at that precise moment, and he knew it was Liam without even looking. He'd done nothing but message him since they exchanged contact details so he could add Liam to his waiting list for rat kittens.

Jamie was almost certain he'd lose interest before they were even born, so he'd grudgingly allowed it. There was no denying Liam loved the rat he already had.

He went to mention that Liam was the clown who'd knocked him arse over tit, but the words didn't form on his lips, so he took another drink and kept that information to himself.

"Are you going to be okay to play tonight?" Markus asked.

Dane reached over the table and gave his arm a consoling pat. Jamie forced himself not to pull away. His friend was only trying to help. "Yes, darling. If you're not up for it, we won't mind."

Markus made a noise in the back of his throat that sounded suspiciously like he did mind. Jamie frowned at him and then answered Dane. "I promised this would not affect the group, didn't I? I'll be fine." He'd secretly hoped both would say it was fine for him to miss the gig, but now it was a matter of principle.

They all drained their drinks. Dane waved at the manager, who was drinking at the side of the bar, his green mohawk flat and brushed to one side. They wound their way through the crowd to the small stage in the corner of the pub. Calling it a stage was generous. It was two pallets duct taped together, with old carpet tiles glued to the top.

The fabric was sticky under his feet, and he bounced on his heels a few times, trying to get into the groove of it.

Nothing helped. He couldn't get into the zone. There was so much history in this pub. So many corners where he and Paul had made out, so many laughs had. He picked up his ukulele, but the weight felt like lead as he put the strap around his neck.

Dane took to the microphone, and Jamie had never been so glad he wasn't the front man. It felt wrong to be playing the ukulele. He was sucking all the happiness from it. The uke created such joyful music that it usually put him in a good mood, but not this time. He scanned the crowd, and two people were missing, making it seem barren.

# Chapter Five

HAVE I Found a Boyfriend?
*L_ofa_Ride*
45K Views. 1 week ago

A half-played game of Coppit sat abandoned on one side of the kitchen table. Selena sat opposite it, her face serious in a way that only those on the wrong side of merry could get. Liam wasn't faring much better.

"Your sympathy skills suck," he said.

She laughed louder and tipped her glass of wine sideways, almost spilling it everywhere. Liam dipped a finger into his own glass and flicked it at her to catch her attention.

"Hey," she protested, wiping her cheek. It was *not* funny. "I've known Frank practically as long as you. Well, okay, since we were pimply, petrified eleven-year-olds just going up to high school. You really thought I wouldn't get an invite of my own? Hell—Frank, Alice, and I get together at least once a month just to talk about you." She jabbed her finger at him and then rolled the dice and moved her counter.

"Well, it's lovely I'm so popular that you feel the need to talk about me behind my back. Maybe Dawni and I need to do something similar." The bottle of cheap plonk between them was rapidly disappearing. They were going to need another… or five. "Stop laughing. He's my cousin, but I didn't get a plus-one."

"You don't need a plus-one. You're the best man. You have an important job, and there won't be any time for YouTube shenanigans." Selena used to enjoy his vlogs when he first started them as part of his media studies degree at university, but she thought he should have long since grown out of it. Party pooper.

"Well, it's not like I'll be banging the bridesmaids, is it? I'm going to prove them both wrong, you know."

"If you pretend a random hookup is someone you're dating, they'll never forgive you." It sounded like she wouldn't either.

"No, nothing like that. I don't actually want to ruin their wedding." He rolled his eyes at her and then picked up the dice and shook them. "But I do have a plan. I met this guy." He thought of Jamie, and a grin formed on his lips. The opportunity was perfect, and he had to take advantage of it. "He's just come out of a long-term relationship, so he's not looking for anything serious. It's a win-win. I can be his rebound. He can be my plus-one."

"You're not taking this seriously. You have to grow up sometime, Peter Pan."

Liam rolled his eyes at her and caught one of her counters on the board. There wasn't a serious bone in his body—a lazy bone, a couple of old broken bones, sure. "This is serious." He was serious about getting Jamie to help him. "We can't all find the love of our life at a lesbian book club." He raised an eyebrow at her. It really wasn't fair that she had. Who did that? "I am determined to take someone to that bloody wedding, even if I have to kill a man and go all *Weekend at Bernie's*."

A notification flashed on his phone, and he grabbed it, disappointed it wasn't Jamie—not that Jamie had replied to any of his messages. Liam wasn't worried, though. He had to let him lick his wounds a little before he made his move. He tapped on the notification and read the last comment on his latest video.

*You didn't find the man of ur dreams :-(*

He inwardly rolled his eyes and ignored it. Sometimes it was too difficult to keep track of the different conversations in the comments, so he just didn't say anything.

Selena groaned and banged her forehead on the table. "It's like talking to a brick wall."

"I'm going to prove you all wrong." He took a slurp of wine and grimaced. "You do know that we're not at uni anymore. We can afford better wine than this." He drained his glass, filled it again, and sighed when Selena tilted hers for a top-up.

"You do know we're not at uni anymore, so you can give up that vlog," she said back, imitating him. "Besides, this is tradition."

"So is a plus-one at a wedding."

He opened Facebook to check Jamie's page and noticed he'd checked in at a small pub that played live music not too far away. He was obviously getting over his hatred of social media. At least a little.

An idea started to form. Liam loved music. He nudged Selena's leg with his foot. "Fancy going out tonight?"

It wasn't quite stalker mode… just yet.

THE DRUNKEN Duck smelled of stale beer, sweaty bodies, and just the merest hint of urinals. Classy. A three-man band played in the corner on a somewhat rickety stage that only just fit the three of them.

They pushed their way to the bar as the music washed over them. It took Liam a while to pick up the rhythm from the chatter of noise. His one good ear struggled to process the different sounds, but once he did, he enjoyed the nimble sound of the instruments and the low, soft voice of the singer.

He stood on his tiptoes and strained to get a better look, but there were too many people shoving and pushing each other as they sung along that he couldn't see them properly. They finally got their drinks. Selena got served quicker than him and handed him a bottle of Bud. He frowned. It wasn't his drink of choice, but it was wet. Liam nudged his way through the groups of people, eyes skimming for Jamie and not finding him anywhere.

When he'd checked the bar and the lounge, he gave up and went back to watch the band. He might as well catch a little live music while he was there. Liam was disappointed but determined to have fun now that they were there. Maybe Jamie was in the toilet.

The last place he would have looked for Jamie was the actual stage. His mouth dropped open, and he had to blink to make sure he wasn't seeing things. Jamie stood stiffly, head down, playing a sunburst ukulele with talented fingers.

He would have laughed out loud at the picture of three grown men playing miniature guitars, but there was tension in Jamie's shoulders, and when he looked up, his eyes were strained, lips drawn. Did it really take someone over two weeks to get over an ex?

Liam recognised the singer as the vet who'd tended to him the night he knocked Jamie over. He rocked out as though he were playing at Wembley Stadium. He exuded confidence and looked much more at home there than he had in Digbeth. Liam didn't recognise the third man, so his gaze shifted to Jamie again.

He nudged Selena and pointed his bottle at Jamie. "That's him," he shouted into her ear.

"He is cute. Great voice too."

Liam shook his head. How could she think that? "Not him, the one with curly hair." She seemed surprised, although he wasn't sure why. Jamie would be a good fit, and he couldn't imagine Alice not liking him, which was hilarious because Jamie didn't seem to like Liam much at all.

They started playing a different song, and it took Liam a second to recognise it because the arrangement was so different. He was impressed when they played a fun and cheerful rendition of "Enter Sandman."

He started to sing along to the lyrics while his eyes roamed the stage, always going back to Jamie. There was a poster behind them of three rats in black suits, with *Rat Pack Rangers* written in large bold font across the top. It couldn't be anything other than the name of their band. It had Jamie written all over it.

# Chapter Six

SWEAT DRIPPED down the side of his face, and he tasted salt as he bit his lips. His playing was terrible. His fingers were wooden, and he kept forgetting chords. The others tried to make up for it, but all he could do was try to get through to the end.

He didn't look at anyone. He concentrated on the music, felt the chords beneath his callused fingertips, and prayed for it to be over so he could go and wallow in peace.

Paul had moved all his things out of Jamie's house, and he'd been surprised at how little there was. Even so, it was empty without Paul there. Jamie couldn't stop picturing him with Tommy.

He shrugged and tried to push it away, but the images haunted him day and night. When he was in bed, he couldn't help but wonder if they'd ever fucked there.

He hoped not, but he wasn't sure of anything anymore. They came to their last song, and he felt giddy with relief and ready for it to be over. The crowd lapped it up, and he smiled with an empty flash of teeth as he put his uke back in the case and slung it over his shoulder.

"I'm heading off, guys. See you later." He went to jump off stage, but strong hands grabbed him around the waist and swung him to the ground.

He gave a yell so high-pitched it would have sent dogs running, and he grabbed on to forearms covered in worn black leather to stop himself falling. He knew who it was, of course. Who else would it be?

"We need to stop meeting like this," Liam grinned as he slid his hands to Jamie's waist.

Jamie noticed that his eyes were two different colours under the harsh light on the makeshift dance floor. He'd never noticed that before, but he had been preoccupied. He pushed Liam's hands away. "Are you following me? You're like a bad smell."

Liam pouted and held on to his chest in mock pain. "And here I am, thinking we're friends now. Hell, we're practically family. We'll be tied by rat family trees soon enough."

"That's a long way off. There are a lot of people before you on my waiting list."

"I'm prepared to wait."

Jamie didn't know what to say to that, so he kept quiet.

"This is my very best friend, by the way. Selena, this is Jamie."

He only then noticed the pretty girl with shiny brown hair tied into a bun, showing off an undercut. She was staring at Liam with a look of concentration and jumped slightly when he nudged her and brought her out of whatever zone she was in.

"Oh, hey. Yes. Good to meet you." She grinned at him and showed a dimple in her left cheek. It was a surprise to see Liam had any friends. Jamie presumed he was too self-centred to be close to anyone but himself. Which was shitty of him, especially as he had helped Jamie that day. He didn't have to, and Jamie still didn't understand why.

Jamie managed to smile at her, and then he heard Dane's voice rise, and he winced. Who was he fighting with now? He turned to find out what the problem was and saw Paul and Tommy. It was like a punch in the gut, and the breath shot from his lungs and left him dizzy. It was the first time he'd seen them together since the split, and it was so much worse than the images in his mind. Fucking he could almost deal with, but the way they stood shoulder to shoulder, Paul's arms crossed in defiance and Tommy with a casual yet claiming hand around his waist, shouted intimacy. It wasn't just sex, and that hurt more than anything he had pictured so far.

Tommy, at least, had the grace to look uncomfortable. Dane, bless his heart, was trying to get them to leave before Jamie spotted them, but Paul wasn't having any of it.

"This is a public house. We can come here if we want."

Jamie's throat seized up, his tongue so dry it stuck to the roof of his mouth. He grabbed the bottle of Bud out of Liam's hand, knocked back half of it, and handed it back. Liam stared at the bottle, ran his finger over the rim where his mouth had been, and took a sip himself.

"Leave it, Dane. He can do whatever the fuck he wants. He always does." Paul always got his way. He'd forgotten that.

Paul and Dane recognised Liam at the same time, and Jamie laughed at how different their reactions were. Dane turned away from Paul, walked over to Liam, and pressed a kiss to his cheek.

"I recognise this clumsy oaf." Dane smiled at Liam. "How's the head?"

Liam touched the back of his head. "It's still there. But the lump has gone."

"Trying to replace us already, are you?" Paul's face was pinched as he scowled at Liam. "A wannabe rock star and his fag hag? How original."

"Leave it, Paul. Let's just go and sit down, have a quiet drink," Tommy pleaded, trying to pull him away, but Paul shrugged him off and stepped forward.

"Tommy's right. Let's not start anything tonight. Sit down," Markus said in a tone that brooked no argument. He pushed Paul and Tommy away with an apologetic look back at them.

"Well, he was a bag full of delights, wasn't he?" Selena said.

"That, my darling, is an understatement," Dane said. "So tell me, how did you two meet properly?"

"I took my rat to a rat show, and guess who was there?" Liam said, grin wide as he poked Jamie in the side and made him jump.

Dane's eyes widened as he put two and two together. "Oh. The infamous rat show. You like rats, do you?" he said to Liam. Then to Jamie, he said, "You sneaky boy. You didn't tell me he was the handsome bloke Jan saw you with. I expect more gossip out of you."

Jamie felt his cheeks burn, and he fought not to look at Liam to see what his reaction was. "It didn't seem important in the great scheme of things." He glanced over at Paul, who was sitting in their booth, and he shivered, suddenly cold. Tommy had his arm around Paul's shoulders and held Paul's hand with his other on top of the table.

A pang of loneliness shot through Jamie's chest. He missed Paul, missed them both. He missed going for a pint with Tommy, missed kissing Paul, missed the way their bodies fit together.

Dane coughed and touched his arm, pulling his gaze away. The pity was back again, and Jamie couldn't deal with it. "I'm going to head home." He shrugged the uke higher up his shoulder and walked toward the door, refusing to look at Liam, who had seen too much already.

A part of him was disappointed that none of them stopped him, but it was what he wanted and what he'd asked for.

He got home to his cat sleeping on the kitchen table. There was a note tacked to his fridge in his mother's handwriting, and it made his blood boil. For fuck's sake, he wished she wouldn't just let herself into his house. She had a key for emergencies, not to let herself in whenever she felt like it. He stomped over to the note, yanked it free, and sent the magnet flying.

> *Jamie,*
> *You and Paul haven't been round for dinner in months. Give me a ring and we can set something up. I wouldn't have to break in if you answered your phone or visited once in a while. I needed to check that you were still alive and hadn't been eaten by the cat.*
> *Love, Mom*

He crumpled the letter in his hand. *Great. Marvellous. Another thing to deal with.* He could just imagine her face when he told her he and Paul had split up. He loved his mother, he really did, but she would make such a big deal out of it and catastrophise it. He was already doing that himself. He didn't need her to do it too.

His cat looked up and meowed but didn't move. He gave her a stroke behind the ear, and she started to purr. "Hey, Stark. Have you been busy sleeping? Looks like it was a hard day for you." He put some biscuits in her bowl and she jumped down and nudged her head against his leg. Then he made his way upstairs to the rat room.

The most exciting thing about buying his own house was being able to install a rat room. He'd hand built a wall of cages to the left,

and to the right were three Savic Royal Suite cages as well as a chest
of drawers he used to keep hammocks, food, and substrate in. There
was a pinboard above, full of rosettes that his rats had won, and it
always made him feel better to look at them. He went to a cage where
five of his bucks lived, opened the door, and scooped out the one
closest to him. Poe was a beautiful black dumbo rat with perfectly
formed ears and a glossy coat. His temperament was outstanding. He
licked Jamie's hand and moved his fingers so he could nibble at his
nails. Jamie stroked between his ears with one finger, and Poe's eyes
started to boggle.

Jamie smiled. Maybe being a crazy old rat man wouldn't be
so bad.

JAMIE WAS so thankful that his job as countryside manager at
Lockstone Chase kept him not only physically busy, but mentally.
He worked hard, sometimes in horrible conditions, but there was a
flexibility not there in other jobs, and no day was ever the same. It
was a godsend as he tried to keep his mind occupied. Sometimes he
wished he didn't have to deal with quite so many people, but overall,
he couldn't think of a job he'd like more. That and Dane were the
only things keeping him sane after Paul split up with him. An image
of Liam flickered through his mind, but he shook it off before it could
take root. He didn't know what to think of that yet.

Their whole friends' group was fractured, and it was exhausting
as he tried to pretend he wasn't hurt or mad and that he didn't care if
Dane and Markus stayed friends with Paul and Tommy. He felt guilty
for the position they were in, and it wasn't even his fault. He wanted
to be petty and demand they stop being friends, but he knew that was
a shitty thing to do, so he kept all his hurt to himself and tried to get
on as best as he could.

Jamie carefully walked through the heathland, minding the
pretty purple budded flowers as he stepped. The wind picked up, and
he shivered beneath his green fleece. He wished he'd put on trousers,
not shorts. Luckily the sun was bright, so it wasn't too uncomfortable.

His body felt heavy and tired as he walked. He hoped that
meant he would sleep that night. He'd taken a class of schoolchildren

around Chasewater, spoken to the RSPB volunteers, spent too long pushing paper in the office, and only now had he managed to escape for the afternoon over Cannock Chase. He followed the natural grassy pathways over the rolling banks, and the long reeds tickled his bare legs. There was less scrub on the ground, and he gave a nod in satisfaction. Introducing the grazing cattle had helped keep the scrub down and gave the heathland a chance to flourish, bringing in so much wildlife from insects to birds.

There was a large black cow in the distance, and he steered himself toward it, stepping carefully through the heath. The birds whistled above him, and he started to relax, letting the crisp, cool air sink into his lungs.

"Jamie, wait, please wait," a voice shouted from behind him, making him jump, not just because he didn't expect it but because he knew whom that voice belonged to. Jamie stood still and took a deep breath, then turned around.

Tommy ran toward him, stumbling slightly over rocky mounds. His forehead was sweaty, and he was wearing jogging bottoms and a baggy T-shirt that did nothing to hide his muscular arms and broad shoulders.

"Ben said you'd be here somewhere, but I wasn't sure I was going to find you."

Jamie wished he hadn't. "I'm at work, Tommy. What are you doing here?" Jamie crossed his arms. He didn't want to deal with this now. This was the one place he shouldn't have to worry about bumping into Tommy or Paul.

Tommy shook his head and sighed. "I just wanted to say I'm sorry. We both are." His voice had a pleading quality to it that grated on Jamie's nerves.

"You've already said sorry. On my answer machine, by text—and I don't fucking care." It was a lie and they both knew it. It wouldn't hurt so much if he didn't care. Tommy had been a constant in his life for so long that missing him was a physical ache. Most of his memories from his teenage years included Tommy, which made it even more painful. He couldn't just blot them out, no matter how much he wanted to.

"We didn't mean for it to happen. The last thing I wanted to do was hurt you." Tommy did look upset, he'd give him that. But Jamie couldn't just forgive and forget. How could he trust Tommy again? He'd shared so many hopes and dreams with him, and he felt… violated. If Tommy could do this to him, then what else could he do—what else had he done?

"You've got a funny way of showing it. We've been friends nearly our whole lives. You were like a brother to me. How could you do that?" Jamie wanted to scream at him or punch him—possibly both. He took a steadying breath and unclenched his fists at his sides.

"It's not like we thought, 'Let's cheat on Jamie today.' We just…. I don't even know. We fell in love. But we didn't know what to do because neither of us wanted to hurt you."

Jamie snorted, his lip curled distastefully. "Didn't want to hurt me? Paul broke up with me in public. Not only that, but he knew how important that day was to me. That doesn't sound like a man who didn't want to hurt me. The opposite, in fact. 'Vindictive' springs to mind."

Tommy winced. "It might look like that, but he was freaking out beforehand. He got it into his head that he had to do it then or he'd chicken out. I know it was a shitty thing to do, and it was a shitty time to do it, but he wasn't thinking clearly."

"I'm so sorry poor *Paul* was having such a hard time deciding how to split up with me. Fuck you, and fuck Paul. Oh wait, sorry—you're already doing that."

Jamie turned around and strode off, hoping Tommy would leave him alone. The anger burned inside him now, and he tried to hold on to it because anger felt better than pain.

"It's not all our fault, you know," Tommy shouted.

Jamie laughed, the sound sticking at the back of his throat like sandpaper. "What the hell do you mean by that?" He stood still and turned around as Tommy walked toward him again. Tommy's cheeks were flushed with anger—what did he have to be angry about? Jamie hadn't done anything wrong.

"Oh, come on. You, Dane, and Markus have been close since uni, with the band and all your practices. Me and Paul, we're always just on the sideline. Rat Pack Ranger groupies. We just got close when you were all doing your thing," Tommy said.

"So it's my fault because I didn't give either of you enough attention? Grow up." What a pathetic excuse.

Tommy let out a frustrated grunt. "Don't put words into my mouth. I *fucking* love him, okay?" It was Tommy's turn to laugh now, and he sounded as unhappy as Jamie was. "I think I've always loved him, but I didn't let myself think about it because you always liked him, and you always get what you want. Fancy job, great house, gorgeous boyfriend." He sounded bitter. "I just locked away my feelings until I forgot all about them. I never expected him to return them."

Jamie didn't want to hear this. Didn't need to hear how much they loved each other. He rubbed the ache in his chest absently. "I loved him too. We were living together. We were serious." He'd thought they were. He loved Tommy as well, not in the same way, of course, but that was why it was so difficult. It was why he couldn't get over it. The two people he loved most in the world, the two people he thought loved him, had betrayed him, and he was meant to sit back and forgive them? He couldn't do it.

Not once had he ever suspected Tommy liked Paul as more than just a friend, and he never guessed Tommy was jealous of his job. It wasn't Jamie's fault Tommy was too scared to pursue a career in countryside management after he was made redundant from his last job. It was as if one bad experience put him off for life.

"This is all crazy," Jamie said. "It doesn't even matter. Whatever you felt, whatever the reasons, what you both did was wrong." Now the can of worms had been opened, Jamie couldn't stop the words spilling out. He'd repressed so many of his feelings because he didn't want to make things awkward for their friends, and he'd not confronted either of them. "Cheating is unacceptable anyway. I can't trust you ever again. I doubt I'll ever be able to forgive you—just leave me alone. Go back to your boyfriend, but don't be surprised if he does the same to you."

Jamie walked off again in the opposite direction, praying that Tommy didn't follow him. He didn't look where he was going and walked into a patch of stinging nettles that sent sharp tingles of pain up his legs.

"Shit," he cursed, hopping out of the nettles and onto a dry piece of dirt.

He hoped Tommy hadn't seen that. He was humiliated enough as it was. His legs were mottled with tiny, itchy red spots. *Just great.* He found a few dock leaves growing next to the nettles and roughly pulled them out of the ground. He rubbed them against the rash on his legs, soothing the irritation. It wasn't the first time he'd been stung by nettles, and it wouldn't be the last.

He glanced behind him, and Tommy was nowhere to be seen. He let out a breath of relief and kicked at the batch of dirt, wishing it were Tommy's face. The dirt was little more than dust and gravel that sprayed in the air as the wind blew around him. It covered him in a fine layer of dust. *Great.* Now he had a stone in his boot.

His phone vibrated. What now? He sighed in frustration. Bloody Liam asking to go out for a coffee. Before he could think more clearly, he texted back, agreeing to meet up. He didn't need Tommy's friendship, and he didn't need Paul's love.

# Chapter Seven

To Fake or Not To Fake?
*L_ofa_Ride*
547K Views. 3 days ago

"It is a truth universally acknowledged that a single gay man in possession of a good pet rat must be in want of a husband—or at the very least a fake boyfriend." Liam watched himself talk on the computer screen, gently swaying in his chair, mindful of Mabel sitting on his shoulder. "I don't know, Riders, am I putting all my eggs into one basket? How do I persuade him to go on a date with me? Ideas in the comments, please." The video was a rare moment of seriousness mixed in with humour. It was odd that he could have a somewhat serious conversation with his viewers... until he realised it was because they couldn't answer back. Then it made sense.

There wasn't much to edit on this video; it was mostly him talking. He just needed to clean up a little, add his intro, and then upload it. It was only six minutes, but he didn't like to ramble too long unless there was action to balance it.

Seven minutes after the video went live, there was a like and then a comment.

*Forget about him, I'll be your Mr Darcy. Let's meet x*

He didn't want to forget about Jamie. He liked a challenge, and he didn't think the comments that were still coming would do any good. But he could at least show his softer side, and who would be able to resist Mabel? Liam reached for his phone, opened Messenger, and sent Jamie another text.

There was no reply straightaway, but Liam didn't expect it. Then he glanced at the clock and cursed.

He was going to be late for his next student unless he got a wriggle on, so he put Mabel back in her cage, jogged outside, and put the magnetic learner driver plates on the side of his car, and a large plastic driving school sign on the roof that incorporated his business name, *L of a Ride*. He was damned proud of the name he'd picked, using a play on *L* for learner driver and his name to come up with it. It was a little cheeky, but it always stuck in prospective drivers' minds.

He arrived outside Tyler's house with one minute to spare. He texted him to let him know he was outside, and the door opened quickly. Liam got into the passenger side, and Tyler sat behind the wheel. He turned and signed, "Hi," at him, and Liam signed back with a smile.

Then Tyler put on his seat belt, did the mirror and signal manoeuvre, and pulled away from the curb, only jerking the car a little.

COSTA WAS nearly deserted. Jamie found a seat at the back and stirred his flat white, glancing up at the door whenever anyone came in. He wasn't exactly sure why he was there. He'd turned into a recluse when Paul and Tommy showed up at the Duck, and he was determined not to speak with Liam ever again, but his last message was intriguing and completely different from the usual jokey ones he usually sent.

Liam strode through the door, wearing his trademark leather jacket, his blond hair brushed messily off his face. His eyes were startling, even from the other side of the coffee shop, and the smile he sent Jamie's way made his stomach twist uncomfortably. Liam waved and walked to the counter. He motioned if Jamie wanted another drink, and Jamie shook his head, cupped his mug, and took a sip. As the hot liquid scalded the roof of his mouth, he hissed and put it down quickly.

Liam came over, a large frothy coffee in his hand, and sat opposite him. "Hey."

"Hi." Jamie didn't want to make small talk. He wanted to know what Liam had to say to him.

"Have you eaten? Do you want a sarnie or a slice of cake?" Liam glanced at the array of cakes on display.

Jamie ground his teeth and shook his head. "Let's cut to the chase. What is it you wanted to talk to me about?" Liam was impossible to offend. He just smiled at Jamie and leaned his elbows on the table.

"You're a rat expert, right?" He took a sip of his coffee, dipped his finger in the froth, and licked it off. Jamie's mouth suddenly felt dry, and he sipped his own coffee.

"I guess. It depends on what you mean by expert."

"I've had Mabel for almost two months now. I've done plenty of research, but going to the rat show opened my eyes. Mabel's diet is poor. I need to find her better food."

Was he serious? "You couldn't ask me that on Messenger? I think you're a big boy and you can buy your own damned rat food." He stood, chair scraping against the floor. Liam shot his hand out and held his wrist in a gentle grasp that Jamie knew he'd be able to pull out of if he wanted. He should. He should tell him to go to hell and go home to his cat. And his rats.

"Hear me out first, please."

He sat back down and pulled his arm away, wrist cold where Liam's hand had been. "Go on, then."

Liam licked his lips. Jamie had never seen him look nervous before. "I really don't know where to start, and I'm scared that she'll end up with a worse diet if I don't have help. Pretty please."

Jamie snorted at him. Was this guy for real? "There are so many resources online."

"True, but I can't tell which ones are best. You want Mabel to be healthy, don't you? Then when I get my new rats, they'll already be on the best diet around. Please?" Liam's blue and hazel eyes widened in his version of the puppy-dog look.

"I'll write you a list," he said dryly, not ready to give in.

"Come shopping with me now. You're not busy, are you? It'll be fun." His voice was low, with a hint of gravel, and Jamie's heart skipped a beat.

"All right, considering we're already here." Now he knew why Liam wanted to meet on the retail park. There was a large pet shop, a Sainsburys, and a health food store within a few minutes of each other.

They went to the pet shop first, and Jamie had to physically drag Liam away from the rats. "No, you can't look at them. It'll only make you sad. Think puppy farms."

Liam grimaced and let Jamie pull him toward the rows of small-animal food. There were a few commercial mixes that Jamie told him to stay away from, and he pointed out a few of the best ones.

"Which do you use?"

Jamie decided he must be in the twilight zone, because there was no other reason he would be with a hot blond shopping for rat supplies. If only it were Paul.

# Chapter Eight

EARLY ON a Sunday, Jamie got the call from Dane at the vet surgery. Someone had abandoned a plastic box with a mother rat and her babies outside their door. Anger burned inside him at the thought. There was no need to abandon any animal. There were so many places they could be taken if someone couldn't look after them properly.

He waited his turn at the reception desk. "Hey, Karen. I'm here to pick up the rats from Dane."

"Jamie, it's been too long since I saw you last." She stood up and ran around the front of the desk to give him a hug. "Come on, I'll take you around the back. He's in the small observation room."

She opened the door for him and shut it behind him. Dane was dispensing medicine into a small pot but turned to grin at him. "Hey, darling, thanks for coming in." He put the medication into a box. "They're through here. I've just put them in a carrier. You can give it back to me later." They walked into a large room where the animals stayed overnight. There were two dogs sleeping in cages and a cat meowing opposite.

Jamie peered in the top of the carrier. The mother was terrified and so skinny. She frantically covered her babes in the strips of fleece they put in for her to use as bedding, then burrowed in next to them until they couldn't see them anymore. There were six kittens that couldn't be over three days old.

"Thank you so much for taking them, darling. The RSPCA are at capacity, but I knew they'd be better off with you anyway."

"It's no problem. They tend to ring one of us breeders if they have rats in need of rescuing, so you've just cut out the middleman. Plus I don't have any boarders at the moment, so I have the room. Any issues?"

"A slight respiratory infection, so I'll send some Baytril home with you, but nothing too bad. She just needs some good food so she can feed those babies, and then some gentle handling."

"Well, I'll take them out of your hair and let you get back to work." He pressed a kiss to Dane's cheek and picked up the carrier. "I'll let you know how they are tonight."

"Thank you, darling."

The hospital cage was set up in his box room, and he had some nice food to tempt the mother. Luckily the kittens all had little white bands on their bellies, which showed they were getting enough milk. He just hoped it stayed that way.

He threaded the seat belt through the handles on the carrier and drove back home. Mommy rat was skittish and didn't like being handled. She wriggled when he lifted her from the carrier to give her a quick look over.

Apart from being too skinny, she didn't look bad. He put her down, and she ran into the plastic house, nose quickly poking out as though she wondered where her babies were. He lifted the fleece out and put them all in front of the house, and she quickly picked them up one by one, carried them inside, and pulled the fleece in after to add to her nest.

Jamie took a few photos and tried to remember how to post them to his Facebook group. It had been ages since he'd used it last, and he couldn't quite remember how.

He'd get some weight on her and give her and her babies lots of love. He'd hopefully find them all good homes. Not everyone wanted pedigree rats, just well-handled pets.

Once he was sure they had everything they needed, he left them to get settled in, wandered back down to his living room, and flicked on the TV. Nothing grabbed him, and he flung the remote across the sofa. *Shit.* He needed to get a grip. His home had lost its warmth since Paul left. He missed seeing him curled up on the chair, watching reruns of *Miami Ink.* He even missed the snarking about the rats and the cat hair.

His phone vibrated, and Jamie checked the notifications He saw that Liam had commented on his post, and he messaged him privately to ask if he could reserve two of the rescue rat babies. Jamie stared at his phone for ages, unsure how to respond. Was he saying it just to stick around, or was he serious?

Whatever it was, Jamie didn't reply. He glanced at the clock on the opposite wall. He'd be seeing Liam in around eight hours for a curry anyway. He still didn't know how that had happened. A moment of weakness after seeing a photo of Tommy and Paul on Tommy's Instagram, perhaps? He should really quit following them, but he couldn't stop himself checking, inspecting their photos, and looking for a reason why they'd done it.

He shook his head. He was truly pathetic.

JAMIE FROWNED when he saw Liam's silhouette through the stained-glass panels on the front door later that evening. He was second-guessing giving Liam his address, but it was too late now. Nerves danced in his chest, and he took a deep breath.

This was a bad idea, but it was better than going to the Duck. Tommy and Paul were at the pub with Markus and Dane, and the thought of seeing them together made him feel physically ill. They were there every time they went out, and Jamie was sick of it.

Usually when couples broke up, they didn't see each other again, but he had Paul shoved in his face at every moment. It didn't help that Tommy was so guilt ridden he kept trying to talk to him.

Jamie couldn't take it anymore. His nerves were shot, and his face ached through the fake smiles. When Liam asked him for a curry, he said yes just to get away from them, to prove that he was over them.

He regretted that now. Through the stained glass on his front door, Jamie saw Liam's blond hair and trademark leather jacket. Nerves danced like moths bouncing head first into a lightbulb. His palms were sweaty, and he wiped them down the leg of his jeans before he opened the door.

By the time he got the door open, Liam was crouched over, stroking Stark. She meowed when she saw Jamie and sauntered inside, brushing against his leg as she did.

"I hope she's yours." Liam straightened up and ran a hand through his hair to push it out of his eyes.

Jamie tamped down the irrational anger he felt at seeing Liam stroke the cat. It was pointless; he wasn't even mad at Liam, not really. He just happened to be the one who was always there, so he got the brunt of it.

"I don't think she'd care if she weren't my cat. But yes, she is. That's Stark." He gave a tight smile.

"She's cute."

For some reason that comment quelled the rest of his anger, and he could breathe again. "She thinks so. I hope she didn't hair you."

"I don't mind. My mom has six cats, so I'm used to it."

That was a surprising revelation. He shifted awkwardly on his feet as he realised Liam was still on the other side of the door. "Do you want… to pop in while I get my jacket?"

He stood back, and Liam stepped over the threshold with a smile, shoulder brushing against his. Jamie shivered and bit his lip. Then he reached back to grab his denim jacket while Liam looked around the hallway with interest.

"Geek, huh?"

Jamie's hackles instantly rose, and he turned sharply to look at him. But he bit back a retort when he realised Liam wasn't making fun of him.

"Is Iron Man your favourite Marvel superhero? Mine's Loki." He frowned for a second. "Although I'm not sure he could be considered a superhero."

Jamie shoved a hand in his pocket and moved on the balls of his feet, unsure what the hell he was doing. "I don't know. Sometimes he's one of the good guys."

"And sometimes he's a very bad boy."

Jamie's stomach quivered, and he jiggled his keys. He wanted to leave before he could deal with it. "I think that's why I like Iron Man. He's a loveable rogue. Ready?" It was a silly thing to say. Liam was waiting for him, after all.

"Almost."

Liam took half a step toward him, and Jamie held his breath as he got close. Was he going to kiss him? That was a bad idea. He was an emotional mess. But he licked at his dry lips, and Liam followed the movements as he rested his hands lightly on Jamie's shoulders.

Jamie should move away from him, but his heart started to flutter, and it was the first time in months he'd felt anything other than a constant ache. Liam stepped up to him and moved his hands around to the back of his neck, playing with the collar of his jacket.

Jamie held his breath and swayed, dizzy with lack of air, and just as he started to close his eyes in preparation, Liam slid his hands around his collar, down the front of the denim, and gave it a tug. "There. You were all twisted."

Jamie let go of the breath, and his eyes shot open, his vision dark around the edges. He stepped back then, embarrassment colouring his cheeks. He cleared his throat and fumbled with his key as he tried to lock the door behind them. *Shit.*

# Chapter Nine

THE TINY hole-in-the-wall Indian restaurant played soft-yet-upbeat Bangla music and was decorated in deep reds and golds. The lighting was soft and intimate, but not too intimate. They were seated at a small round table near the back wall, poppadoms and wine in front of them—but not the awful stuff he drank with Selena, something that cost a little more than £3.99.

It was difficult to stop smiling. Jamie was tense and distrustful, and he kept glancing at him as he ate his poppadoms. Liam pretended not to notice. He'd finally shaken Jamie out of his well of self-pity, even if it meant he was grumpy again. Liam knew Jamie had expected a kiss, and he'd wanted to give him one. He liked kissing, and he was good at it, but he needed to draw Jamie in and get his mind off his awful ex and terrible former best friend.

Alice would love him. Selena even liked him. *He* liked him.

He cracked his poppadom, spooned some mint sauce on a section, crunched into it, and licked the sauce off his lips. "How are the rescues?" Liam said between bites. He'd noticed Jamie hadn't replied to his messages.

A small smile flickered across Jamie's mouth, so fleeting Liam almost missed it. It was different from the snorts, unhappy laughs, and tense smiles he'd received before. There was less of an edge. It seemed more genuine.

Something unfurled deep in his stomach, something he hadn't felt in years. He grabbed his glass, took a gulp of wine, and let the alcohol settle his stomach.

"They're good. Momma rat is doing a great job. Babies are getting fed."

"I'm glad. Am I allowed to reserve two of the kittens?" He raised an eyebrow.

"You were serious? I wasn't sure."

"Completely serious…. Why wouldn't I be?"

Jamie shrugged and ate the last of his poppadom without looking up again. Liam found he missed those small looks. He pulled his chair farther into the table and spread his legs out until they pressed against Jamie's.

Jamie jumped, and his knees banged into the top of the table. Liam held on to his wine glass, trying not to laugh. "I'm deadly serious about the rescues. Reserve two girls for me… if there are any girls."

"There are. Okay, I will." Liam didn't move his legs away from Jamie's, and neither did Jamie.

Their empty plates were replaced with a chicken balti for Jamie and a bhuna for him. They fell into easy silence as they ate.

Perhaps if his previous dates had gone like this, they would have lasted longer. It was the first ordinary date he'd gone on since university, and he wasn't terrible at it.

"Is this a date?" Jamie suddenly asked, looking up, fork midway to his mouth. Was he a mind reader?

Giving Jamie the trademark smirk he used on his vlogs, Liam stared at him, taking in his curly hair, the light scruff on his cheeks, and his dark-brown eyes. Jamie was really good-looking. Liam knew that on the surface, but in that moment, it was like a shove to the chest.

"Why? Do you want it to be?" He put as much charisma into his answer as he could and pressed his leg harder against Jamie's. When Jamie pulled away and hooked his feet behind the chair legs so Liam couldn't reach him, Liam's joy dimmed. Had he taken it too far? Most people couldn't resist his smouldering looks.

Liam fidgeted with the stem of his wine glass, suddenly overinterested in what his fingers were doing. Jamie was taking a long time to reply. When the silence became too heavy, he rolled his shoulders and felt the muscles click. Then he looked up. Jamie was staring at him, head cocked to the side, brow furrowed. He wasn't exactly frowning, but he wasn't happy either.

"Very presumptuous of you, isn't it? I don't know why you're here. You've seen me at my worst. You should be running for the hills. I'm a mess right now."

"And you think I'm much better? I crashed into you running from my date at Zombie Brum City." Jamie gave a shaky laugh, which was what Liam was aiming for. He didn't need to know all the details of what happened. "I figure neither of us are looking for something serious, but we could both do with a good distraction. I could be your rebound guy."

"I don't know." Jamie moved his legs back under the table, and they pressed against his. Liam bit the inside of his cheek to keep from smiling. His head might not be sure, but his body was.

"Come on. You get to not be the pathetic ex, and I get to casually date a guy who's not looking for marriage and a white-picket fence but will make my friends and family see me as a grown-up." The white-picket fence didn't make him shudder like it used to, but he pushed the thought aside and nudged Jamie's leg. "Plus you're hot."

Jamie rolled his eyes as though he didn't believe it. "Yeah, right."

Paul had obviously done a number on Jamie's confidence if he didn't know that. The thought of spending so much time with one man wasn't as off-putting as long as Liam knew that man was Jamie. He pictured them having fun—in the bedroom and outside it.

"Couldn't hurt, I suppose." Jamie looked back down at his curry.


LIAM DROPPED Jamie off, expecting to go straight home. But Jamie hesitated, his hand on the door handle, reminiscent of that awful day in the car park. "Do you want to see the rats?"

He wasn't going to look a gift horse in the mouth. Liam turned off the ignition and undid his seat belt. "I'd love to."

He'd only seen as far as the hallway when he was there earlier, but he'd already learned so much about Jamie, from the female cat called Stark to the superhero figures that lined the wall next to the living room door.

Liam wanted to see more of Jamie's house so he could learn more about him. He usually only wanted to see the bedroom, and then he never cared about getting to know more than what would drive them wild in bed.

"Would you like a drink? Tea?" Jamie shifted awkwardly on the spot, hesitating in the hallway.

"Please." He didn't really fancy a drink, but he could tell Jamie needed something to compose himself with. Liam followed him into the living room, sidetracked by the bookcase and the ukulele he'd seen him play at the Drunken Duck hanging on the wall beside it.

"How do you take your tea?"

"Milk and three sugars." It was always interesting to see what was on another person's bookcase. He could tell so much by what was there. The whole living room screamed *Jamie*. He glanced at a shelf full of graphic novels, most of which were Marvel.

Jamie laughed. "Three sugars? Really?"

"What can I say? It's how I stay so sweet." He gave a wink and turned back to feeling the book spines to find which ones Jamie had read the most. He pulled one out—Poppy Z. Brite's *Exquisite Corpse*—and turned it in his hand. He slid it back and then came to a whole corner dedicated to an author called Lynn Flewelling.

One shelf was entirely made up of environmental textbooks, which made him wonder what Jamie did for a living. He frowned. They hadn't really talked much. Liam was there when Jamie had his heart broken, and he knew he was feeling down in the dumps, but he didn't know the usual details. Liam wasn't good at that side of dating. If he could just take Jamie to bed, he could guarantee he'd do better there.

While Jamie was in the kitchen, he looked at another shelf and discovered a whole pile of gay romances. Smirking, he picked one up. The two men embracing on the cover were hot. He flicked through it for the naughty bits but ended up getting hooked on their story and jumped back to the beginning.

Jamie gave a little cough, and Liam fumbled and looked up. "You found my guilty pleasures." Jamie nodded at the book. He didn't seem embarrassed about them, so Liam wasn't worried about being caught snooping.

"Oh yeah. I was looking for the rude bits." He grinned and put the book back. "I got hooked onto their story instead. I didn't even realise there were so many gay romance books."

"There are if you know where to find them. Kettle's just boiled. I'll make that tea."

The kitchen was a long galley that didn't have much room, but everything was well placed and homey. Jamie fetched mugs from the cupboard above his head. One was the *Doctor Who* TARDIS, and the other said *Kiss the Librarian* and had fake blood splatters down the side. Liam should know what that was from, but it escaped him, and he didn't want to ask, so he glanced around the kitchen instead.

It wasn't a show kitchen by any means, but it was bright, clean, and felt very much like home. There were photos attached to the fridge with tacky tourist magnets. They were curling slightly at the corner, and some of them had liquid or food splatters on them. He peered closer, interested in Jamie's life more than he thought he would be.

He recognised most of the people—Dane, of course, and the guy with the beard who was in Jamie's band. There were also some of Tommy and another photo hidden behind the others. He parted them to see what it was and then wished he hadn't.

Jamie and Paul kissing. Jamie had his eyes closed, hands in Paul's hair, and Paul was glancing sideways at the camera, shoulder at a funny angle, as though he were the one taking the picture.

Liam's chest felt tight, and he absently massaged it as he stared at the photo. He jumped a little when Jamie seemed to appear right beside him with a bottle of milk in his hand.

"I didn't even know that was still there." He bit his lip, and the confidence from earlier disappeared. He reached around him and put the milk back. Then he took the photo off the fridge and shoved it in the rubbish bin.

"You didn't have to do that." It was nothing to do with him if Jamie wanted to keep their photo on his fridge. He had no right to feel weird about it. They were just two blokes having a good time, nothing serious between them.

Jamie picked up the two mugs of tea and handed one to Liam. "Here. Do you still want to see the rats?"

"Of course I do." He blew on his tea for something to do. "Lead the way," he said, trying to lighten the mood.

It was odd to be walking up the stairs of a man's house, carrying a cup of tea, knowing they weren't going to end up in bed together. Still, it didn't prevent his cock from stirring with interest. It was either that or how Jamie's arse looked in tight denim as he walked up the stairs in front of him. His tea wobbled, and he slowed down before he could spill it. Jamie opened a door to a small box room and turned the light on. He placed his mug on the sideboard, so Liam put his next to it, and then they stood side by side next to a small cage.

Jamie picked up a bag of yoghurt drops and crinkled the plastic. "Hey, girl," he said softly. "Do you want a treat?" A nose appeared out of the purple plastic house, and a small, thin rat gingerly came to the bars and took the treat.

"She's tiny." Liam had seen the photos, but he hadn't expected her to be so small.

"She is, but she's on a good diet now, and she's being a great mom. Look, if you peer in here, you can see the kits." Liam placed his head right next to Jamie's, and their hair brushing against each other's made him shiver. The nest was dark inside, but he could see squirming.

"I see them."

He couldn't contain his excitement, and he looked at Jamie, their faces so close he could feel Jamie's breath on his cheek, and they shared a smile. All he had to do was tilt his face up, and they could be kissing. Liam licked his lips and wondered what Jamie would taste like. Arousal curled in his belly, telling him to turn it up a notch and kiss him, but his head said something else.

He straightened up and looked back into the cage. "I definitely want two of those."

"You win. I'll reserve two for you. Want to see the main rat room?"

Liam's eyes widened, and he nodded. A whole room full of rats? Of course he wanted to see.

"Come on. Show me the rats." He did an awful "show me the money" impression, making Jamie laugh, and when Jamie casually touched his arm, the small movement sent tingles down to his fingers.

The rat room was impressive. There were rosettes pinned to a board, and each cage had hammocks, tubes, and toys. When Jamie turned on the light, he heard rustling, saw whiskers twitching, and lots of eyes peered at him through the bars. Some of the does climbed the bars closest to them, after attention.

"They are so sweet." He walked over to a cage, gently stroked a paw that was poking through the bars, and laughed softly when they tried to grab him. Another rat scurried over and pushed the first one out of the way to see what was happening.

"Want to give them a yoghurt drop?" Jamie opened a tub full of treats and offered it to him. He took a handful and made sure each rat had one. "I know people say not to feed them through the bars, but I can never help myself. That's Piper you're feeding there, and her sisters Prue, Phoebe, and Paige." Liam vaguely recognised the names but couldn't quite think where they were from.

"Want to hold one?" Jamie opened the doors without waiting for a reply. There was no hesitation as furry little bodies climbed up his arms and onto his shoulders. He didn't end up with just one but had three running along his shoulders and diving down his T-shirt. He winced as their nails left scratches.

Jamie murmured to the rats in the next cage but didn't get them out.

"Easy," Liam murmured as he steadied him with a hand and one of the rats scrambled along it and up onto Jamie's shoulder.

Jamie was in his element, standing there with a rat on his shoulder, and Liam thought Paul was a fool to let go of him. He might not be looking for a happily ever after—didn't really believe in them—but even he could tell Jamie was a catch.

Jamie's breath hitched, and his eyes widened and zeroed in on Liam's lips. With any other man he would smile, smirk, and draw more attention to them, but it didn't cross his mind to try that with Jamie—not here, not now.

His heart beat so loudly that it echoed in his bad ear. He couldn't let go of Jamie's elbow, didn't want to lose the connection, however small it was. The air was charged around them, so thick he could feel the weight of it on the back of his tongue. Could Jamie taste it too?

The rats expertly ran down his arm toward Jamie and he pulled him closer. A gasp of air left his mouth, and one of the rats ran around his neck, her tail hitting him in the nose.

Liam chuckled, each movement sending waves of desire to his rapidly filling cock. "Cute," he said, unsure if he meant Jamie or the rats. He hadn't expected this level of attraction.

Jamie's arm was smooth beneath his touch, a light layer of dark hairs tickling his fingertips and the play of muscle tensing beneath. Gently he moved his hand up Jamie's forearm until he was clutching his bicep, and as his fingers tightened, he leaned in, finally pressing his lips against Jamie's.

# Chapter Ten

THE BLOOD rushed through Jamie's veins as Liam's warm lips found his. The tender press of their mouths made Jamie gasp, sucking in air from Liam's lungs and surrounding himself in the scent and feel of him.

His head told him not to do it, but his heart, still broken and so sad from constantly hurting, wanted it more than he wanted air to breathe. Relief swept through him and made him giddy, and he had to grab hold of Liam's waist to make sure he didn't fall flat on his arse. He expected a hard kiss, one full of nothing but heat and the promise of sex. This was something else—something he didn't have the words for.

Liam nudged his lips open with his tongue and curled into his mouth until Jamie groaned and tightened his hands in Liam's T-shirt. He could get lost there and never have to think about Paul again.

Usually he'd close his eyes and let the sensations overtake him, but he didn't trust that Liam wouldn't disappear, so he kept them open, and his heart pounded when Liam did the same. Liam's eyes were heavy lidded and bright, and Jamie could see that the left was a pale blue with a few hazel flecks and the right was hazel with a few blue flecks. He groaned again, and Liam swallowed the sound. His five o'clock shadow scraped against Jamie's chin in a way that would mean he'd feel it afterwards. He wanted to feel it.

Absently Jamie realised that the rats were still on their shoulders, but he was too far gone to pull back. He didn't need Paul or Tommy. Liam dug his fingers into his arms, and the kiss deepened. Jamie could kiss Liam forever. His lips were soft and full, his tongue hot and heavy. When Liam wrenched his mouth away, Jamie gasped, lips glistening.

"Wha—?"

Liam gave a strangled cry, back bowing backwards, his face pinching in pain. He scrambled for the hem of his T-shirt. "They're climbing up my back," he said as he twisted around and tried to grab the rats out of the back of his T-shirt without hurting them.

Jamie bit back a laugh—they'd all been there—and put Piper back in the cage. Then he rescued Liam from her sisters. He turned Liam around and shoved his hands up his T-shirt, feeling the hot, tight skin under his palms before he felt wriggling furry bodies. He scooped them up, gave them each a kiss, and put them in their cage. "Little witches," he said affectionately.

"It's not funny," Liam said, his swollen mouth pouting as he tried to rub the marks on his back.

Jamie hadn't even realised he was laughing, but Liam's pout just made him laugh louder. It probably wasn't that funny, but it had been so long since he'd laughed that he couldn't help himself. "It really is. Let me look at your back." He pulled Liam's shirt up and winced at the bloody welts. That must hurt. "You're fine. Come on, Bowie, let's go to the bathroom, and I'll get the disinfectant wipes." The nickname fell off his lips so naturally he didn't even notice he'd said it.

"Bowie?" Liam asked, pleased.

Jamie gave an awkward shrug of the shoulders and grabbed an old shoebox out of the cupboard under the sink to look for wipes. "Just slipped off the tongue. Sorry."

"Don't be. I like it. Though technically he didn't have two different-coloured eyes, just one dilated pupil." Liam grinned. *Know-it-all*, Jamie thought but couldn't bring himself to be mad at him.

"You're taking it too literally. Come on. Take the shirt off."

Liam pulled the T-shirt over his head, revealing pale, toned skin and a six-pack that made Jamie's mouth water. His fingers itched to touch.

There was a small covering of blond fuzz over Liam's chest and down to his belly button, and it was difficult to drag his gaze away. When he did, he expected Liam to be giving him a knowing smirk, but his face was tense, nostrils flaring.

Jamie touched his side with a shaking hand and pushed Liam to turn around so he could see his back. He winced at the bloody rake marks and dabbed them with disinfectant wipes. Then he ran his fingers gently down Liam's spine, needing to touch. His skin was covered in goosebumps, and Jamie almost pressed a kiss between his shoulder blades, but Liam twisted around and grabbed his T-shirt.

The easy flirting from before was gone, and Liam's eyes were guarded, his mouth tense. Jamie didn't know what had happened.

"I had fun tonight. We'll get together soon?"

Jamie nodded, unsure what to say. Liam's words were confusing after the intimate moment of before. He needed to remember that they were just meant to be having fun—no feelings involved. So he took a deep breath and pasted on a smile, now in control of his own emotions and feeling better.

IT TOOK a long time to stop feeling Jamie's hands on his bare skin. He knew he'd given Jamie mixed messages, but he underestimated how much such a simple touch would affect him.

Jamie was an unexpected find, and the more he thought about him, the more excitement and nerves battled inside him. Jamie was all contradictions—one part snark, one part sensitivity. That kiss…. It had left him reeling. Even thinking about it made his lips tingle and his cock stir. He'd expected to feel the same emotions he had with his usual hookups, which was why it scared him when Jamie's touch got to him so much.

He lay on his bed in just his boxers, trying to drift off to sleep, but his mind was too busy—and even after brushing his teeth, he could taste Jamie in his mouth. Lazily he scratched the hair below his belly button and gently slipped his hands beneath the waistband. His cock was hard, and he groaned when he grasped the root. Images of Jamie danced over his closed eyelids, and as he tightened his grip, he pictured it was Jamie stroking him. For once, he wasn't in a rush to get off, and he moved his hand slowly, gripping his length, pressing his thumb against the tip with each upward motion.

Heat coiled in his balls and drew them up, his legs fell open, and he thrust slowly into his fist. The orgasm was unexpected, slow, and sweet. His breath hitched and stuttered, his hand froze, and then his limbs turned to liquid. It took a while before he was able to clean up and pull himself under the covers, but he fell asleep easily, and Jamie's awkwardly sweet smile was the last thing he pictured before he drifted off.

LIAM YAWNED and his jaw clicked as he read through the comments on his computer. His views had gone down slightly, which was worrying. He wasn't sure what to do to bring them back. Well, he did, but he was concentrating on just Jamie right then, so he wasn't looking for new dates.

"You're feeling guilt." Selena sat cross-legged on the floor in the middle of the living room.

"Don't be stupid. I don't have anything to feel guilty about."

"Of course not. So… does Jamie know about the vlog? The wedding? What exactly did you say when you put your idea forward?"

Jamie shrugged. "It's not important. I just said I wanted something more serious than a one-night stand, but nothing too serious. He agreed—it benefits him too. Did you know that he has to put up with the ex whenever he and his friends go out?" Liam couldn't think of anything worse than having to hang around with people he didn't like.

"It sucks. I don't envy him. But I still don't get how this casual-dating thing really benefits him."

Was she being obtuse on purpose? How could she not see it? Both he and Jamie understood it perfectly. "He gets to look as though he's over Paul. It's mutually beneficial."

"I'd feel better if he knew all of the details."

It really wasn't that difficult. It was a win-win situation, and no one needed to know the ins and outs.

"It's not about how you feel." She opened her mouth to argue, and he held out his hand. "Forget it. We're already going on our first official nondate, and nothing you say will change it."

"Where are you off to on this nondate?"

"Just to his mate's—you know, the singer? Dane?" She nodded but didn't seem impressed. "It's more of a casual get-together. You and Dawni should come too."

"You're inviting me along on your date?"

"It's a get-together—shindig, party, whatever you want to call it. You don't have to come if you don't want." He folded his arms and stared until she lowered her gaze in guilt.

"I want to, I'm just trying to get my head around all this. So… you basically get sex on tap, and you just have to pretend to be his boyfriend?"

"It's not like that. Why do you have to lower the tone?" She had to take everything in the wrong direction.

# Chapter Eleven

JAMIE AND Ben had both spent the entire day in meetings or at their respective desks. Neither of them was made for office life, and by the time they switched off their computers, they were almost climbing the walls.

"I don't see why meetings can't be held outside. Why do they want to be indoors when we've got all that on our doorstep?" Ben grumbled as he grabbed his coat.

"We can only dream. Unless they need to see something in the flesh, then we're stuck in boardrooms and behind those evil things." Jamie gave his computer a glare. He loved working outdoors, but he hated being in the office and going to meetings that dragged on for eternity. Walls were not his friend.

"Next week will be better," Ben said. Jamie nodded. They both had a full week outside. They had volunteers out litter-picking to manage, newt habitats needed to be built, and there was always more scrub clearing that needed to be done and people to organise. "I am ready to get out of here," Ben said as he grabbed his jacket. "You coming to the pub?"

Jamie blinked. He'd never before forgotten about their usual routine, not even when he was first with Paul. "I'm really sorry. I've got plans tonight."

Ben's smile dimmed. "No problem. Next time."

"How do you fancy a night of board games at Dane's instead?" Jamie offered before he could think too deeply about it. Ben knew all his friends from the occasional event and night out, but they didn't socialise that often. Perhaps he could talk to Ben and forget Liam was there. A shiver raced down his spine. *Fat chance.*

Ben laughed loudly. "Board games? Is that what they're calling it now?"

Jamie shook his head with a forced laugh as he picked dirt out of his fingernails. How had he gotten so dirty when he'd been indoors all day?

"Seriously. Board games, beer, you know Dane and Markus. You can meet… my new boyfriend. It'll be fun." He wasn't sure whom he was trying to persuade. It was the first time he and Liam were going out with their friends as something more than two strangers who kept bumping into each other. Nerves made his gut clench. It would be nice to have another friend there who was completely his and not Paul and Tommy's too.

"You sure I won't be crashing? I don't want to crash your party."

"It's not. You know most of them anyway. This way you get to meet Liam." He felt a fraud saying it, but he didn't know what else to call him. They'd spent time together, they'd talked about a relationship of sorts, and he came around nearly every week to watch the rescue rats grow from little jelly beans into inquisitive hyperactive kits.

They'd had no repeat performance of that kiss yet. Part of him was relieved for it, another disappointed. If he could get lost in Liam, then he wouldn't think about Paul.

"Okay. Give me the address. What time should I be there?"

JAMIE PICKED up Liam and finally saw his flat, which was mostly taken up by a huge aviary cage he'd adapted for Mabel and her soon-to-be sisters, Gertrude and Maud. Jamie rolled his eyes. Apparently Liam got a kick out of old-lady names. He picked up Selena and her girlfriend, Dawni. It was obvious from their easy mannerisms and how their hands found each other that they were smitten with each other.

Jamie glanced at Liam and pushed his hands in his pockets as they walked around the side of Dane's house and into his back garden. "Should we be holding hands?" Liam whispered as he watched Selena and Dawn.

Jamie shook his head and curled his fingers into fists. "No, that's not necessary." Liam seemed to think it was, and as they rounded the corner, he attempted to pull his hand out of his pockets, but Jamie refused to move.

"Come on," Liam said.

"There are the lovebirds," Dane interrupted, BBQ tongs in hand, obviously misinterpreting the scene.

Jamie glared at Liam, his face burning in anger as he tried to pull away. Liam tutted at him, put an arm around his shoulders, and pulled him in to his side. "We can't get enough of each other."

"Well, come and get a drink." They gathered on the patio, Selena already talking to Markus and Ben as Markus shuffled a deck of cards.

A small dog yapped and ran toward Jamie. "Speedy G." He dropped to his knees, relieved to use the dog as an excuse to step out of Liam's arms. He wanted to hold his hand, but he wanted Liam to want it too, which just pissed him off. One official date in, and he was already making it more than it should be.

Markus persuaded Selena and Dawn to join them in a game of cards, and Jamie concentrated on the dog, pointedly not looking at Liam. Speedy wriggled onto his lap, looking for kisses with his long tongue. He laughed and lifted him up so he could reach Jamie's face. Liam crouched down next to him and stroked Speedy's head, close enough that Jamie could smell his spicy cologne and feel the breath against his cheek. His stomach tightened as he inhaled. He loved the smell of good cologne on a man.

Paul and Tommy walked through the back door and into the garden, holding hands. Jamie felt the laughter fall from his face. He tensed as Liam's gaze drifted toward them. It shouldn't hurt this much.

Liam grabbed his hand and pulled him to his feet. They held hands as they walked toward their combined friends at the table. Liam didn't let go when they reached them, and Jamie's palm started to sweat. He let out a breath and tried to relax, entwining their fingers like he'd wanted to do earlier. Liam shot him a smile and squeezed. Then he turned back to the conversation.

The banter flowed over Jamie's head. He tried to keep track of it, but he could feel Paul's glare dig into his back. He glanced around, but Paul quickly looked away and leaned his head on Tommy's shoulder.

Tommy just looked constipated. If Jamie weren't so tense, he would have laughed.

"Okay?" Liam whispered, lips grazing his ear and making him shiver. Jamie chanted *rebound* in his head and managed to get himself under control.

"Yeah. It's just cold," Jamie said.

Liam nodded even though he must know Jamie was lying. The shiver had nothing to do with the weather.

"Snap," Markus shouted, making Jamie flinch. Then he realised they weren't playing poker, but a game of Snap. He laughed at them, feeling lighter, and pressed his shoulder into Liam's. He could do this.

"Son of a—that's the third hand you've won. You're a card shark," Selena said.

Jamie raised an eyebrow. "Can you even call it a hand when you're playing Snap?"

"It's a valid card game. I say you can." Selena took everyone's cards and placed them in a neat pile. "We should play Monster Crunch! next. It was my favourite game as a kid." She leaned over and snatched a game from the pile she'd brought with her.

"See? You have to match the monster with the one on the screen, and then use your hand sucker to slap it."

"So it's basically pairs?" Ben said. Then he took a sip of his beer, hiding his smile.

"Yes," Dawn said dryly as she poked Selena in the ribs. "She likes games that come in pairs."

"It's so much more sophisticated than boring old pairs. Isn't that right, Liam?"

"You have to excuse her. It's the only board game she ever wins." Liam stuck out his tongue at her, and Jamie didn't even have to pretend to smile.

"That's such a lie. I win at... I win at marbles too," she said desperately.

"Marbles are not a board game," Dawn said with an affectionate roll of her eyes that made Selena pout.

"None of you know anything. Come on. I demand you all play. You gay guys are picking on the lesbians." She stuck her tongue back out at him.

"Hey, they're not picking on me." Dawn laughed and gave her a one-armed hug.

"And, err, not gay," Ben said with a slight blush. Jamie hadn't known that, not that it mattered either way.

"I'm sorry, hon. I just presumed because these lot are all so flaming. It's good not to be the only ones who don't find these guys attractive. We'll have to stick together." She didn't miss a beat, and Ben didn't even get offended.

"Dane, get your arse over here. We're playing Monster Crunch!" Dane had left the burgers long enough to talk to his neighbour over the small fence that separated their gardens, conveniently getting out of playing. The neighbour was holding a boy about five or six years old, and they were talking rather seriously. They jumped and looked over when Selena shouted.

"Games?" The boy's eyes lit up, and he looked longingly over to their side of the fence, then at his dad, then back again. To be fair to him, their side of the fence did look more fun.

"It's a kids' game. He's welcome to play," Selena said. His dad hesitated and looked at Dane.

"Why don't you both come over for a burger and a few games?" Dane said.

"I don't want to impose…," he said, but his son was getting restless in his arms.

"You're not, darling," Dane said, and much to Jamie's surprise, he held out his hands to the boy, who leaned over trustingly, and his father let him go.

Jamie had never seen him talk to kids before—animals, yes, but not children. Dane put the boy down and walked with him over to their table. "Come on. You're not imposing. We're just playing board games and eating our weight in cow."

"If you're sure…." The neighbour jumped over the fence and followed Dane and his son.

"Puppy!" The boy saw Speedy G under the table and quickly got to his knees, ignoring all the adults in favour of the dog.

"Arthur." His dad went to pull him away, but Dane placed a hand on his arm to stop him and got down with the boy himself.

"This is my dog. His name is Speedy Gonzales, but we call him Speedy G for short. Do you want to throw the ball for him?" Speedy G was wagging his tail and licking the boy's hand. Dane pulled a tennis ball from nowhere and handed it to the kid.

The kid's father smiled awkwardly at them. Jamie reached around Liam and held out his hand. "Hey, I'm Jamie. Nice to meet you."

"You too. I'm Cal, and that's my son, Arthur. We moved in next door a few months ago." He glanced at Markus, and his gaze travelled down his body. *Interesting.* Jamie looked at Markus, who was sitting rather tensely, likely pretending not to notice how good-looking Cal was. Jamie bit the inside of his mouth to stop himself from smiling.

If he concentrated on them, he could almost forget Tommy and Paul were there.

"You should key his car if he parks over your driveway. His driving sucks," Markus finally said with a wink.

"I heard that." Dane shot them a glare and went back to watching Arthur throw the ball.

"It's lucky you know a very good driving instructor. You need lessons, Dane, you come to me." Liam gave Jamie's shoulders a squeeze. "I am going to save the burgers because I think they're burning." He looked over at Paul with a curl of the lip. Then he kissed Jamie's cheek, and the small touch sent a thrill through his entire body as Liam sauntered over to the bar BBQ.

Jamie's shoulders relaxed, and he was able to join in the conversation without waiting to see what Paul would do. Liam might have only kissed him in pretence, but pretend caring was better than being alone in a crowd.

"I am never going to get to play Monster Crunch!" Selena looked longingly at the game, sighed, and then promptly got up to get the best choice of burger.

"It's okay, babe. I'll play with you when we get home. I'll even let you win." Dawn wiggled her eyebrows suggestively, and Selena started to blush.

Jamie went to join Liam to say something witty and fun and show Paul he was over him and didn't give two hoots that he was there. But the hum of conversation slowly died down, and the hairs on the back of his neck stood on end. His stomach flipped, and he turned around, already sensing whatever it was wouldn't be good. Even Liam's smile had dropped from his face, and he clenched the tongs tightly.

It became all too clear once he turned around and saw Paul sauntering toward him, Tommy following sheepishly behind, trying to grab hold of his arm. Jamie braced himself and watched Paul with disinterest. It was funny how he used to feel so breathless when he looked at Paul, but in that moment, with Liam manning the burgers and their friends milling around in the garden, his heart didn't hurt quite so sharply.

A tang of regret sat on the back of his tongue, and annoyance made his skin itch. It was difficult to remember why he'd fallen in love with Paul. His heart felt broken, stuck together with old chewing gum and ukulele strings, but it hadn't stopped beating. Loving Paul had been difficult and stressful, sometimes wonderful and tender, but always one-sided.

Now that he wasn't in the thick of it, he could see that, and maybe soon his heart would catch up with his mind. In the meantime he had a rebound boyfriend willing to help him forget.

"I heard *you* were now the new boyfriend." Paul aimed it at Liam. "He's not had enough of your drama, has he?" Anger crackled with each word as Paul spat them out. Jamie didn't understand why he was so angry. He'd dumped Jamie, not the other way around.

"Come on. Let's get a drink." Tommy glanced at Jamie with part regret and part longing.

Paul made a scoffing sound. "What? I'm just saying. If he's got another bloke, then everyone can stop being so pissed off at us." His eyes settled on Liam.

"Don't make a scene. I think you'll have to agree that we've all done our hardest to keep out of your drama and not take sides," Dane said, stepping away from Arthur and the dog with an apologetic eyebrow raise at Cal.

Sensing the tension, Cal walked over to his son and started to play with the ball to distract him.

Jamie shrugged with a casualness he didn't feel and saw the frown on Dane's lips and the hidden tension beneath his easy stride and fluid movements. "I'm not angry at you," Jamie lied, and they all knew it. "All I'm doing is trying to get on with my life."

"Here's your burger, just how you like it," Liam said as he handed him a loaded plate. Jamie glanced at the monstrosity and pulled Liam in for a quick kiss, tasting grease and fried onions on his lips. The truth was Liam had no clue how he ate his burgers—but neither did Paul.

"Mmm. Thanks, Bowie." He took a huge bite, but he would have eaten it no matter what was on it just to see Paul so pissed off.

Liam pulled away slightly and said to Paul. "Help yourself to burgers and hot dogs." He hoped Liam spat on them.

"You're just trying to rub our face in it." Paul yanked his shoulder out of Tommy's grasp, and Jamie laughed around his burger and swallowed quickly. "And we'll still be on the naughty step waiting for you to let us leave."

"Rub what in your face, exactly? Are you a complete dickhead? You're the one who cheated." What did he want? For Jamie to watch him, lovestruck and heartbroken? He was not going to let Paul see that, and he was doing his best not to feel it.

"Maybe you and Paul should leave," Dane said to Tommy, who frowned but nodded. "Paul, darling. The world does not revolve around you. Stop being such a little selfish shit. You did a crappy thing. At least have the decency to be embarrassed about it."

"You're going to drop us—maybe not today, but soon. We just fell in love. It was wrong to cheat, I get that, but Jamie doesn't make it easy to love him."

Jamie flinched at his words and wondered what it was exactly that he'd found so difficult. He'd loved Paul with everything he was, gave him so much…. What was difficult about that? His face ached from keeping the emotions off it, but for some insane reason, Liam looked right through the mask and saw everything. How did he have the ability to know him instantly while Paul apparently never did?

"I'm really sorry. Come on, Paul," Tommy said as he dragged him away. Jamie had a feeling he was sorry for more than Paul's outburst that evening.

He didn't relax until they'd left the garden and Dane followed them out. Liam brushed the back of his hand against Jamie's, and he jumped.

Dane poked his head out of the back door, and his eyes landed on him. "Jamie, darling, can you help me find the Doritos dip?"

He frowned because Dane knew exactly where it was. "It's in the cupboard at the side of the fridge."

He shook his head. "I looked there already."

Jamie sighed, handed his plate to Liam, and followed him into the house, where he opened the cupboard and shoved the dip into Dane's hand. But Dane didn't even glance at it. He just slid it onto the worktop.

"Are you really all right?"

Jamie blinked as realisation dawned. Oh. That's what it was about. "I told you I was. Liam is nice." He winced at how insipid that sounded but pasted a smile on his mouth and pretended everything was fine.

"I meant because of Paul, but you do have a valid point. This isn't like you, to go from one man to the other. I'm worried. You don't get over someone that quick. Your reaction to Paul says it all."

He winced. Dane had seen through his blank face too. But Jamie forced himself to keep eye contact though he started to blush. "It's still new with Liam. No one likes to hear from an ex that they're hard to love. It knocked the wind from me. With Liam…. You were there the night he crashed into me. Sparks flew, what can I say? I might still be hurt over Tommy and Paul, but life goes on. We're just having fun. You understand?"

Dane gave a dry laugh. "Darling, I'm the epitome of just having fun. You know that, but it's never been your style." It was hard not to look away. Dane knew him too well, but he kept their eyes locked as he responded.

"Maybe I'm taking a leaf out of your book." It sounded hollow to his ears, but Dane eventually nodded, patted him on the back, and then grabbed the salsa and walked back into the garden.

# Chapter Twelve

HE PARKED near Liam's flat. The air in the car thick was with tension, his pulse like fire in his veins. He gripped the steering wheel, turned off the ignition, and twisted to stare at Liam.

Liam's body was tense beneath the artful lounge and smouldering look. Jamie spotted the twitch in his jaw, the heat in his eyes, and the way his chest rose and fell a little too hard. His T-shirt was stretched tight over his chest, the logo on the front half-obscured by his open leather jacket. Did he ever take that damned thing off?

Jamie swallowed. Why were they always in the car for awkward conversations? Liam had been the perfect rebound boyfriend so far. He'd held Jamie's hand and soothed away the rawness of seeing Paul. Now it was his turn. His nerves felt brittle—with one sharp movement, they'd snap and he'd crumble like a deck of cards.

It had been a long time since he'd done this with someone new, and first-time jitters made him want to crawl out of his skin. First times were never how they were described in romance novels. In Jamie's experience, they were always awkward. He'd become used to sleeping with the same man, knowing what he liked, how he looked.

Liam lived in a converted terraced house at the opposite end of Lockstone from Jamie and had precious off-road parking. Cars were parked bumper to bumper on the pavements on either side of the road, so he truly was lucky.

He wet his dry lips with his tongue, and Liam followed the movement with his eyes. Strangely that was all it took to calm his nerves. Jamie peeled his fingers from the steering wheel and concentrated on the soft glow of the streetlamp outside.

He'd thought of saying so many things on the drive over—rehashing old stuff like rules, boundaries.... But sitting there in the dark with Liam waiting patiently next to him, none of that mattered.

Paul didn't want him, but Liam did. Liam, who didn't usually want anyone for more than one night, wanted Jamie tonight, tomorrow, next week. Who cared about a year from now? By then he'd be long gone, and hopefully the feeling in his chest with him.

"Aren't you going to ask me in?" He forced himself to look at Liam and was glad he did. When he wasn't trying to layer on the charm, there was a raw vulnerability to Liam that Jamie wished he could see more of.

Liam's mouth dropped open and then morphed in one of his trademark smiles. He opened the door and put one leg out. Jamie's breath stuck in his throat as he waited. "Are you coming inside?"

Heat uncoiled inside him like a spring, and he let out a shaky breath, yanked the door open, and locked the car behind him. Three long strides and he was chest to chest with Liam. He was an inch shorter, so he had to tip his head back slightly as Liam leaned over and kissed him.

It was nothing like their first kiss. It started out deep and became all-consuming. Liam ran his hand through Jamie's dark curls, and he shivered at the sharp bite of pain as he wrapped them around his fingers and angled the kiss exactly how he wanted it. Jamie swayed toward him, and their chests touched.

LIAM SHUT his front door behind them, pushed Jamie against it, and crushed him as he devoured his mouth and shoved his thigh between Jamie's legs, urging him to thrust.

*Fuck.* He felt good, but kissing wasn't enough anymore. All night he'd given Jamie teasing touches and fond looks to help with the pretence, but he'd driven himself crazy instead. He needed more than fake touches. He needed something real and harsh—something he could taste.

When the room began to spin around them, he pulled back. Jamie's mouth glistened, and his eyes were heavy lidded with desire. Satisfaction curled his lips. That look was for him, not Paul, and Liam wanted to make Jamie forget that fucker's name.

This was where he came into his element. If there was one thing he was good at, this was it, and he would make sure Jamie knew it firsthand.

Jamie leaned his head against the door, his mouth open and swollen, glistening with saliva. Liam's heart skipped a beat at such a wonderful sight, and when Jamie blinked at him, his gaze finally focusing, Liam smiled—that slow half smile that made his viewers weak at the knees.

Liam leaned in for another kiss, distracting him as he undid Jamie's fly, then pushing his jeans and boxers down his thighs. He gasped into Liam's mouth, and Liam couldn't stop the grin forming around the kiss.

Jamie's cock was hard to the touch, his balls heavy and hot. Liam had to taste more than just his mouth. He ripped away from Jamie's lips, dropped to his knees, and pressed his nose in Jamie's neatly trimmed pubes. He was gorgeous. Standing there mostly dressed, with just his cock out, he made Liam's heart race and his ears roar.

Jamie's hand thumped against the door. His cock was already dripping precome, and Liam tasted a droplet on his tongue and let the flavour explode in his mouth with a salty earthiness that he could very easily get used to. They both groaned.

He sucked the cock into his mouth, hollowing his cheeks, and listened to the change in Jamie's voice, doing his best to drive him to the brink. Jamie let out a strangled grunt and gave a stuttering thrust with his hips. Liam's cock was painfully hard, trapped in sinfully tight jeans. He rubbed his palm against himself, but it wasn't enough.

"Please," Jamie said. Liam rolled his eyes upward, caught his heated gaze, and almost came on the spot. He pulled off Jamie with a pop and stumbled to his feet. That usually never happened. He was always in control.

Jamie's eyes bored into his as though stripping him to the bone while keeping him fully clothed. His gut clenched, and he pushed Jamie around until he faced the door and Liam didn't have to stare into those all-consuming eyes. He pulled Jamie's hips until his arse jutted out. That was better. This he could do.

His breath was harsh against the back of Jamie's neck. He yanked Jamie's jeans all the way down, felt the firm globes of his arse, and imagined how it would feel to push between them.

His legs went weak, and he draped himself over Jamie's back, wishing the T-shirt weren't in the way of the open-mouthed kisses he pressed against his shoulder blades. He grabbed the supplies from his jeans pocket and then stood straight so he could free his cock. He shuddered when it hit the cool air.

He wanted to get naked, wanted to strip Jamie until there was nothing between them, but that wasn't how he did sex. He did fast, hot, and sexy, not slow, tender, and heartfelt. He forced himself to do what he knew, knowing they'd both feel good. Jamie didn't want that extra stuff from him, and he didn't know how to give it anyway.

He rolled on the condom with shaking hands, then squeezed some lube down Jamie's crack, fingers quick and efficient as they loosened him up. Jamie made small mewling noises that made Liam's cock twinge, and as he sank into the tight heat, his own grunts joined them.

Jesus Christ. Jamie was unbelievably tight. The ring of muscle twitched around him until he saw stars. "God," he said, laughing because he'd never felt so… much before. Jamie pushed out his arse, grabbed the door handle with one hand, and pressed his other palm flat against the door.

Liam set a brutal pace—fast, hard, and sweaty, thrusting his hips unevenly, the door jingling each time Jamie slammed against it. The room was full of their gasps, the scent of their sweat, and the tender scent of them combined.

It didn't take much to push him over the edge, and when he felt himself coming—that delightful tingle as he teetered over the edge—he fisted Jamie's cock. He came seconds after Liam did and tightened around Liam's softening cock. Jamie's legs failed him, and they both ended up on the floor, breath harsh, eyes blown, and skin cooling in the summer air.

*Jesus.*

# Chapter Thirteen

IT WAS confusing how all-consuming a fake relationship could be. Perhaps if he'd put the amount of time and effort into Paul as he put into making sure people believed his and Liam's relationship, Paul wouldn't have strayed.

They walked shoulder to shoulder along Birmingham Canal, having a couple of drinks on the way. The bars overlooking the water were jammed, people spilling out onto the pathways and up the spiralling steps across the water. They took the scenic route until finally they reached Hurst Street, the hub of the gay village.

Birmingham was a thriving city, but Hurst Street was something special. It sounded ordinary, but there was so much history there. The Victorian Back to Back houses restored by the National Trust stood proudly on the corner. There were LGBTQ+ bars that first opened when it was just a warehouse district and the gay community was looking for a safe place to belong. It was also home to the Hippodrome, where he and Paul had seen the Royal Ballet.

He pushed the thought away, not wanting to ruin the night. He was feeling nostalgic and sentimental. The gin he'd drunk had dulled the edges and brought the ordinary into minute focus. He smiled when a drag king walked by, his hips swaying as he walked in four-inch stiletto heels. Jamie admired the way his short-cropped hair sparkled with red glitter and how his corset cinched his waist, yet made him look masculine at the same time.

It was Friday night, and Hurst Street was alive with queers. His spirit always lifted when he was there. Music pumped out of the Village Inn, and there were men glittering in sequins or dressed in leather, and everything in between. The music was infectious, and the loud, cheesy melody of the cabaret cut into the summer evening.

Liam suddenly pushed him against a wall. The rough red brick was like sandpaper through the back of Jamie's T-shirt and scraped deliciously against his spine. He sank into the kiss with a laugh as catcalls and wolf whistles called out around them. It was easy to forget about Paul and the reason they were doing this.

The night of the BBQ unleashed something inside him. He'd expected sex with Liam to be good—he was gorgeous, after all—but he hadn't expected it to be mind-blowing. That only happened between the pages of the books he read. If rebound sex was this good, then he needed to remember to have more of it.

They stumbled away from the Back to Backs, high on music, sex, and alcohol. They were meant to be getting the drunk train back, but they were having such a good time that they'd decided it was worth splashing out on a taxi.

"Shall we go to Nightingale's?" Liam's voice buzzed with excitement, and it made Jamie feel it too.

"We might as well make that taxi worth it."

They veered off Hurst Street and onto Kent street and joined the queue of people already waiting to get inside.

It had been so long since he'd been to Nightingale's that he'd forgotten how huge it was. The dance floor was vast, already full of writhing bodies moving in time to the beat. Liam dragged him into the throng and pulled him close as they danced.

When Jamie was drenched in sweat and his throat was so dry he thought he would swallow his tongue, Liam went to the bar to fetch them bottled water, and he chugged down at least half in one go.

"It is you! Liam!" someone shouted, though the music swallowed most of the sound.

The guy pushed through bodies on the dance floor to get to him, ignoring Jamie completely. He beamed up at Liam with adoration in his eyes. Jamie knew Liam got around, but he didn't expect one of those hookups to find them in a club as huge as Nightingale's.

"It is you. Oh. My. God." Liam froze, tightening his hands around Jamie's waist. Jamie waited for an introduction but didn't get one. He shrugged it off. Liam probably didn't remember his name.

"I watch your—"

"That's so nice of you. I appreciate it. Thank you so much. But I'm busy right now," Liam said with a tense smile that didn't reach his eyes. His old hookup looked at Jamie for the first time, eyes widening, and Jamie wondered if he had something on his face.

"Is that…?"

"None of your business," Liam said and slung an arm around the stranger's shoulder. He held one finger up to Jamie, promising to be back, and then led the guy toward the bar.

He was back within seconds, and he pulled Jamie back onto the dance floor. But the ease of earlier had disappeared, and Jamie wasn't quite sure how to get it back.

Apparently it took hot, sweaty sex to ease the tension that had fallen over them. When they got back to Liam's flat, he pulled him out of the taxi and up the stairs, not giving him a chance to go home.

Jamie didn't mean to fall asleep once they finished—it was an unspoken rule that once they had sex, one of them would leave.

When he woke properly the next day with his body aching and stomach itching because he hadn't cleaned up, he was tangled alone in Liam's sheets. He touched the other side of the bed and it was cold.

He sat up, brushed his hair back off his face, and frowned. He was still naked, so he looked for his clothes and found his boxers and T-shirt. Unable to face putting on tight jeans over a sticky body, he padded barefoot out of the bedroom.

He heard faint music from the kitchen, and he followed the sound to find Liam singing along softly to the iPod in the small docking station on the corner of the worksurface. Liam stopped when he heard Jamie and gave him an awkward smile.

"Morning," Liam said. "Do you want a sausage sandwich?"

His stomach growled, which made Liam laugh, and some of the tension in his shoulders disappeared. Jamie smiled sheepishly at him. "Morning, and yes, please." The *please* turned into a long yawn. Jamie rolled his shoulders and heard them pop.

The music continued to play, but Jamie didn't recognise the band. They played so many different covers he was always interested when he heard something new.

"Who's playing?"

Jamie put six sausages under the grill. "His name's Phase. He's this punk-rock pianist. He's more underground, so not many people have heard of him. He actually comes from Birmingham, as many of the greats do."

"An Ozzy fan, huh?"

Liam shook his head. "No, Judas Priest, obviously." He gave a wink.

"Phase doesn't sound much like Judas Priest." Jamie felt lighter now that Liam was talking without any tension.

"I have an eclectic taste in music. He's more… Antony and the Johnsons."

"I'll have to look him up. Do you mind if I shower?" Jamie wanted to ask if they could shower together but thought that might be too much too soon.

Liam shook his head. "No, course not. Towels are in the airing cupboard. Do you want to borrow some clothes? I know we hadn't planned on… last night… you staying over."

"Thanks."

The sausage sandwiches were done when he was finished in the bathroom. He smelled like Liam's shower gel and was wearing his clothes. The jogging bottoms were too long in the leg but tight around the hips, and the T-shirt was an old band T-shirt with the arms and neck cut out. It didn't escape his notice that the image on the front was of the singer Liam had been listening to in the kitchen.

Liam carried their plates to the living room, and they settled on opposite ends of the sofa. Jamie took a bite. Liam's feet were so close. It only took a tiny movement, and they were touching. Liam looked at him and smiled—which made Jamie smile too.

"Are you doing anything today? Do you want to watch a film?"

"I have to go home at some point and feed the animals, but I'm free for a while." He put his empty plate on top of Liam's on the floor.

Liam beamed at him and then leaned over and squeezed his knee. "What do you want to watch? I have Netflix, or you can look at the DVDs in there."

Jamie got up, kneeled on the rug in front of the TV, and opened the cupboard next to it. He whistled. Liam had an impressive collection—TV series, films, and then… terrible films.

"Seriously? *I Bought a Vampire Motorcycle?*" The front had a motorbike covered in spikes rearing up onto its back wheel, a group of people cowering behind a cross beneath. Liam laughed, and the sound warmed Jamie's insides and made his stomach flutter.

"I love trashy films," Liam said.

"Me too. But in this case it was more because I had a crush on Neil Morrissey."

He handed the DVD over to Liam, and he put it in the player as Jamie curled back up on the sofa. When he sat back down, he sat next to Jamie, arm across the back of his chair. Jamie moved his feet to curl on the other side and pushed his shoulder into Liam's side.

# Chapter Fourteen

Is THIS What Dating Is?

*L_ofa_Ride*

1 day ago. 85K Views

His parents' living room was full of cats and knickknacks. Photos of Liam and his sister through various awkward stages of their childhood adorned the walls, and the sofas were worn but perfect to nestle into. He sat in comfortable silence with his sister while his dad made dinner. Wednesday nights were always his nights to cook, and Liam hadn't been over for dinner in much too long.

Dumbledore, a velvet grey cat that had adopted his mom over ten years earlier, lay sprawled on his lap, so comfy Liam worried he'd just slide off, which had happened in the past. He meowed and batted Liam's arm, demanding a stroke, and Liam automatically scratched behind his ear and sent the cat into a purring frenzy.

With his free hand, he checked his phone. Only YouTube notifications popped up, and he grunted and scrolled past them. Nothing from Jamie.

Frank would be pleased. Jamie was turning into the perfect companion. Liam hadn't even missed having sex with random men.

Another YouTube comment popped up, and he grunted in irritation.

*He's no good for you—it should be me—I had it all planned out*

Some of his viewers could be a little intense.

His sister jabbed his knee with her foot to get his attention, and the cat took that as an invitation to jump off his lap and onto hers. Traitor. He looked up. *What*? he signed one-handed, pointing his index finger at her and shaking his hand.

She rolled her eyes in exasperation, and he was instantly transported to their childhood. *You're such a twat,* she signed back, which was amusing to see in sign. *What are you doing?*

Despite the sniping and the eight-year age gap, they were close. He'd always felt protective of her.

Bethan's light-brown hair had a natural white streak that she dyed a myriad of different colours. Today was bright orange, not the best colour she'd ever used, but it probably got fewer stares than her natural hair. He couldn't believe she was at university.

"I met this guy." He signed as well as spoke, used to doing both because his dad was hearing and it had become a habit.

He'd practised how he was going to tell his family, subtly let it slip in that he was dating, and his sister walked into his plan perfectly. Bethan's eyes widened, and she poked him with her foot again, making the cat grump. She bounced in her chair and signed for him to give her details. He caught her up on Jamie—the version he wanted them all to know—and tried to ignore the weird feeling in the pit of his stomach.

Beth stared at him open-mouthed. *No way.*

"Yes way." Beth cocked her head to one side and stared straight at him. She stared at him for so long that it unnerved him. Could she tell it was all a lie?

She tutted at him and signed rapidly, so fast that only years of growing up with her and speaking BSL with his mom since he was a baby let him keep up.

"I know what I'm doing. Just because I don't date doesn't mean I don't know how."

She watched his hands with a frown and butted in. *You used to date. I remember you bringing that guy home your first year of university.*

Liam's skin went clammy as he thought back to Richard. "My one and only ex? How do you even remember that dick?" The hairs on his arms stood on end, and he shivered. He tried never to think about Richard, let alone talk about him.

"Dinner's ready," their dad called, making him flinch.

The lamp in the corner turned on and off again, and he heard his dad talking to Alexa. Bethan saw the light flicker and got to her feet, knowing that meant it was time for dinner. The joys of having Alexa. They walked slowly to the door, and then Liam darted forward so he could get to the table first.

Bethan ran after him and grabbed his T-shirt and pulled his hair so he wouldn't sit in the seat they'd always fought over as children. He sat down, victorious, albeit with a sore scalp.

Their mother rolled her eyes and pointed at him. "When will you grow up? You were too old to fight over a chair when you were twelve, and you're too old now." Her speech was slow and precise, the cadence flat, but her hands were confident. Dumbledore brushed around her feet, and she leaned down to stroke him.

Liam grinned and stuck out his tongue at Beth. They all knew it wasn't about the chair but about making sure Beth had as ordinary a childhood as possible. Part of that was teasing her rotten. He'd let her win when she was five, but by the time she was seven, the glory was going straight to her head....

She sat opposite him with a glare. Then she smiled wickedly, and Liam had a second to wonder what the hell she was going to do before she tapped their mom on the shoulder and outed him. Fucking outed him. Damn little sisters and second languages. They should never have taught her to speak.

His mom's pale blue eyes widened, and her mouth dropped open with a loud yelp. "Dating?" she asked as though she didn't believe it.

He kicked Bethan under the table, and she gave him the finger. Why did he always feel like a little kid when they both went home to visit?

"It's not serious. Don't get too excited." A funny feeling went through him as he said it, as though he were adding another lie to a pile of lies. Bethan raised an eyebrow but wasn't mean enough to disclose exactly what he'd told her—thank God.

He glanced quickly at his mom, but she was standing behind Bethan, so she hadn't seen the hand signing, and their dad was busy plating up.

He went to say something else, but his phone vibrated in his pocket, and he couldn't not look. It might be Jamie.

The smile spread across his face instantly. All for show, of course. Beth shaped her fingers into a heart, which would have been sweet if she hadn't followed it by pretending to stick her fingers down her throat in a gagging motion.

"Didn't I say to you when she was born that I would prefer a puppy? Is it too late to send her back and get a dog?" Despite his grumbling, he couldn't stop his good mood.

His dad put a plate of bread and butter in the middle of the table and slid greasy homemade egg and chips in front of him. Nothing tasted better than his dad's chips.

"Have a piece before your sister licks the butter off them out of spite," he said as he ruffled her hair. Liam grabbed a slice of bread and butter and stuck out his tongue at her again.

"So tell us about this boy and how he's different to the others?" his dad said.

Liam groaned. Of course he was listening.

# Chapter Fifteen

THE PUB was relatively quiet as Jamie waited for Markus. Dane sat opposite him, giving him a look. Not just any look, but The Look. Jamie hated Dane's Looks. But they were blessedly free of Paul and Tommy, which he was very thankful for. He was sick of always being on high alert because of them. He just wanted to go out and relax like he used to.

Markus came back from the bar and slid three pints onto the table. "Get that down ya." He sat next to Dane. Jamie remembered how he felt the last time he sat like this, but now he felt… happy.

"So where is the luscious Liam?" Dane wiggled his eyebrows and took a sip of his lager.

"We're not joined at the hip, you know." Except they had been for the last few weeks. Rebound sex was the best.

"Really? That's not what I see," Markus said, giving him a kick under the table.

"You're all knobs. Besides." He looked at his watch. "He'll be here when he drops his last student off." He felt the heat flush over his cheeks when he admitted it. He needed to get a grip.

Liam's hours were all over the place, as he fit them around when his students needed lessons, which meant he spent a lot of weekends and evenings working. It was frustrating, but oddly enough, they managed to make time for each other easily. When the relationship was fake, there was no worry about making it work.

Markus whistled. "He must have some kind of superpower to make you smile like that." Jamie hadn't even realised he was smiling.

"I'm not smiling," he said, but he really was. He dipped his finger into the froth on top of his lager and sucked it clean. He was one of those odd people who liked the froth.

"Don't you think it's too soon to be so loved up?" Markus asked. He and Liam must be doing a good job of pulling the wool over their eyes if they truly thought the two of them were loved up.

Dane snorted. "Don't be daft. Besides, it's not like he has to marry the guy, just have fun. Don't sit around pining after Tommy and Paul."

"I'm not pining after them." He said it too quickly, and they both gave him a long, unnerving look but chose not to press him further.

"Aren't you glad Liam knocked you over outside Brum City now, darling?"

"Then came to your rescue at the rat show," Markus finished in a sing-song voice. Jamie winced as he thought about it, still puzzled why Liam had stuck around. "And don't get mad at me for saying this—I wasn't sure what you saw in Paul. I like him enough. He's one of the guys, but he was way too…." Markus looked at Dane.

"He was high-maintenance," Dane finished. "He was too highly strung for you. Or you were too laid-back for him."

"But he's right for Tommy?" Jamie didn't understand that. He and Tommy were similar in many ways. They'd both studied animal care at college and university, they had similar habits and tastes…. What did Tommy have that he didn't?

"I didn't say that. What they did was shitty, and there's still a very large part of me that hopes they crash and burn just because they betrayed you, which is not okay." Dane said it with a smile, but Jamie knew he meant every word. It meant a lot.

"It's good to know there are still vengeful, vindictive friends in the world." Jamie picked up his glass. "Cheers." They all clinked glasses.

"Hey all, what are we celebrating?" Liam asked as he walked over to the table, looking deliciously rumpled. He had his jacket slung over one arm, and his hair fell messily around his face. Jamie smiled at him and shuffled farther along the bench. Liam slid along the bench, placed a firm hand on Jamie's thigh, and leaned in to kiss his cheek.

"What on earth are you wearing?" Dane asked, his eyes fixed on Liam's chest once he sat back.

"What do you think of it? It's my new uniform." He turned to Jamie and snorted a laugh, unable to keep a straight face. The logo was a rainbow with a car driving over it. In bold writing across the top it said *L of a Ride*, the *L* red like learner plates. Jamie burst out laughing. It was ridiculous, but if anyone could pull it off, it was Liam.

"Is that really the name of your business, darling? Tell me, do you get anyone looking for more than driving lessons?"

"Oh God," Jamie said. "I can just see it now." They all laughed, but Liam just shook his head and rolled his eyes at them.

When the chuckles finally left, Jamie leaned over and whispered against his ear, "You can give me an L of a Ride when we get home." Liam moved his head sideways and gave a dirty grin.

# Chapter Sixteen

"LIAM AND Jamie sitting in a tree—" Selena sang before he kicked her chair under the table and made it wobble. "Jesus Christ, watch what you're doing. I could have fallen and cracked my head open and *died*." She shook her finger at him and waggled her eyebrows.

"Yeah, right. There's not enough room in this kitchen for you to fall off." It was more comfortable in the living room, but they always gravitated toward the kitchen, even when they shared a house at university.

"So I take it your plan to get that coveted plus-one to Frank's wedding is working?"

It made him jump, as he'd almost forgotten about that. He didn't know why the thought didn't fill him with quite as much excitement anymore.

"It's going very well, thank you very much."

"Oh, something meaty for the vlog, then?"

He clenched his jaw and forced himself to smile. That's what it was about, wasn't it? No point getting angry at Selena when she pressed him about it. "Very meaty." He cupped his dick for added effect, and she pretended to vomit.

"He's a sweet guy. Too sweet for you."

"What's that supposed to mean?" He frowned, trying not to be hurt.

"You're going to break his heart. I know it."

"Don't be daft. I'm his rebound, remember? He's just using me to get over his ex." It was the best kind of relationship. "Did I tell you that I pick up my new rats from Jamie's today?" He said it as a distraction, but he couldn't hide his excitement.

"That's brilliant. Let me know when you and Jamie are about next week, and we can do something. Maybe we can double date." She snorted and gave a huge belly laugh that resulted in tears.

"It's not that funny."

"You don't understand. It really is. Who would have thought you'd be dating, let alone double dating? That's one thing you would never even put on YouTube."

TODAY WAS the day Mabel either got two new sisters or turned into a rat killer. Liam wasn't entirely sure which way it would go, but he was trusting Jamie not to let Mabel kill anyone.

Liam spent the day frantically cleaning Mabel's cage and reading up on introductions, and he was still freaked out. How did people do this without having a Jamie to hold their hand?

"There are a few different methods. The newest craze is to put them all in a small carrier so they're forced to be together and there's not a lot of room for fighting." That sounded scary.

"Which one do you do?" He was nervous something could go wrong and was glad he didn't have to do it alone.

Jamie grinned at him, and the skin at the corner of his eyes creased. He kissed Gertrude's belly, and she wriggled her little body against him. She was desperate to get down and play, and she wasn't nervous at all. They'd handled all the babies from the moment Jamie rescued them, and they'd turned into healthy, confident little rats. Maud sat on Jamie's shoulder, her eyes boggling, and she ground her teeth in contentment.

"I'm old-school. When I first started out, the bathtub-and-vanilla-essence method was all the rage, so I just stick to what I know. Jan switched over to it and likes it, though."

"I don't know. It sounds brutal to me." Mabel squirmed in his hands as though she knew something big was going to happen.

"Well, I don't have a bathtub, but the hallway should be okay? It's neutral territory, there's no place they can get out, and I'll put a towel down to catch any ratty raisins. You'll help, right?"

"That's what I'm here for. Rat Whisperer to the rescue."

They shut themselves in the hallway and knelt on the floor. Jamie put down the babies first, and after a second, Liam took a deep breath and put Mabel down. She sniffed the air and walked toward the babies. When she was close, she jumped on Maud and made her squeak. Liam squeaked too, his body tensing as Mabel flipped the babies over. He couldn't watch.

"Mabel," he shrieked, heart stopping, just waiting for the bloodshed. This was going to go horribly wrong. He pictured a ratty murder scene and shuddered.

Jamie leaned over and touched his shoulder. "It's okay. There's no fur flying, and she's not using teeth, just showing them who's boss."

Liam let out a breath. Sure enough, Mabel had stopped trying to beat them up as they all chased each other around.

"It's going well. Trust me," Jamie said with a smile as he tickled Maud when she climbed over his knee.

"This is going well? I'm about to have a heart attack." Gertrude jumped on the spot, vibrated her ears, and jumped on Mabel's back. They were such odd creatures.

"I had this one rat called Cinnabon. She hated every new addition I tried to add to the mischief. She attacked them all, bit, drew blood, and was downright evil. It didn't matter how much vanilla essence I used, what neutral space I introduced them in. The only thing that worked was deep cleaning the whole cage and popping them all back in together before she realised. By the time she did, they all smelled the same, and she left them alone."

"I'd seriously have a heart attack."

"Nah, you wouldn't."

Jamie leaned over, mindful that he didn't kneel on a rat, and kissed him. Jamie's lips were warm and tasted like tea. He pulled Jamie back for another one when he tried to move away.

They took their time making sure the rats were comfortable with each other, and when Jamie thought they were ready for it, he put them in Mabel's cage. He added the younger two first and let them explore. Then he popped Mabel back in and watched in case she became territorial.

Maud and Gertrude were into everything, exploring the *Ghostbuster* hammocks, running through tubes, and climbing the bars until they reached the Sputnik at the top. "This is good, right?" Liam glanced at Jamie.

"It's great." He threaded his arms around Liam's waist and squeezed.

"Phew. I'll make a brew. Want to watch a DVD while we keep an eye on them? We can see what's on Netflix, or you can find another horror flick."

While Jamie knelt to rifle through his DVDs, Liam went to the kitchen. It felt very domestic having Jamie in his flat.

He'd memorised how Jamie had his tea—builder's tea with one sugar. He carried them back to the living room and placed them on top of the fireplace, as he didn't have a coffee table. Jamie was sitting crossed-legged on the floor, piles of DVDs around him. "*Critters.* I used to love that as a kid." He waved it a little.

"Me too. Want to watch it?"

"Sure." They curled up on the sofa, and barely fifteen minutes into the film, Liam drifted off to the motion of Jamie's breathing.

# Chapter Seventeen

I F*CKED Up—I'm Sorry
*L_ofa_Ride*
2 days ago. 127K Views

Liam realised quite suddenly, after one drink too many, after hanging with Jamie's friends and the exes who just wouldn't take the hint, that he didn't enjoy being around them. Dane was lovely and Markus seemed like a decent bloke, but they reminded him of the deal he and Jamie made. It was completely irrational—they didn't even know about it. Yet seeing them always brought it to the forefront of his mind.

Jamie seemed happy on the stage and happy off it. Only occasionally would he see Jamie stare at Paul for a second too long with tension in his eyes. Liam's heart lurched when he saw those looks. He didn't enjoy seeing him in pain.

He couldn't be angry at Jamie if he was still pining after his ex. Jamie hadn't promised Liam anything, and that's how he wanted it. He couldn't go changing the rules now. And why would he want to?

The ukulele looked hilarious in Jamie's arms as he danced his fingers over the strings, plucking expertly. He was loose limbed and feeling the rhythm as he bopped to the music, and Dane's voice was loud and smooth. Liam remembered back to the first time he'd seen Jamie play. He'd been so sad, the music a foreign body instead of a part of him.

The Duck was jammed as usual, and although the guys had a table reserved for them, Paul and Tommy were sitting there. He'd rather pull teeth than sit with them, so Liam joined the crowd on the tiny dance floor, moshing along to the songs and belting out 80s ballads with the best of them.

Jamie looked like Slash, his hair frizzing with sweat, curls bouncing as he rocked out. When their set finished, he propped up his uke, jumped down off the pallets, twisted his way through the crowd, and made a beeline for him. He grinned, face flushed, body still vibrating from the music. He walked into Liam's arms with no hesitation, tilting his face back for a kiss. Who was Liam to deny him?

When they pulled apart, Paul and Tommy joined them, more's the pity.

"Just like old times, right?" Paul said, his mouth moving into some attempt at a smile. Tommy stood next to him, nursing his beer. Liam felt a little sorry for him, but not too sorry. Paul hadn't cheated alone.

"Not quite like old times," Jamie replied as he took the Diet Coke out of Liam's hand, so reminiscent of their first night together in the Duck. He moved the glass until his mouth pressed exactly where Liam's had been, and it was enough to make Liam's cock stir in his jeans.

It hadn't escaped Liam's notice that Dane and Markus barely spoke to Paul and Tommy. Maybe they'd had enough of their shit as well. He didn't know why they didn't tell them to take a running jump. And although Paul seemed to thrive on the tension, Tommy shrunk further and further in on himself.

Liam's vision tilted as two huge arms snagged him around the waist, lifted him, and spun him around. Liam let out a cry, thankful he hadn't been drinking as his stomach was left behind.

He didn't need to look and see who it was. Those arms could only belong to one person. Jamie stepped back and saved the Coke.

"Frank, you bastard, do you want me to vomit on you?" He shoved him away with a laugh and slapped him on the back so hard his wrist ached.

"I thought that was you over here. Where you been? I haven't seen you in ages." His cheeks were flushed, and eyes were slightly glazed. He'd obviously already had a skinful.

Liam hadn't spoken to Frank in months, not since he'd been given that ultimatum. He glanced at Jamie, who was watching them with interest, and shifted on his feet.

"Alice let you out, I see?" Liam teased, and with a forced smile, he carried on. "Jamie, this is my cousin, Frank. Frank, this is Jamie… my boyfriend."

Frank's eyes widened in acknowledgement, and he stared at Jamie from head to toe. "Oh. *The Boyfriend?*" He gave Liam a wink, but he was so drunk he blinked both eyes. Then he shook Jamie's hand enthusiastically.

"How much have you had to drink, Frank? I should call Alice to pick you up." He wanted to get him away from Jamie before he said something stupid.

Frank scoffed and pointed out his mates at the other end of the bar. "We're not even started yet. Is he the guy you decided on for our wedding? Is he good enough to get you a plus-one? We'll have to see."

Liam winced. Too late. "Stop being a knob. You're drunk. I already told you I'd met someone. I just didn't want to subject him to you quite yet." He let out a forced laugh and desperately wished Frank would just disappear… at least until the wedding.

Jamie's smile was pasted in place as though he weren't quite sure what was going on, but he knew there was something brewing beneath the surface. "Who's getting married?" he asked.

Liam tried to remember exactly what he'd said about his family, but it was as little as possible. Selena and Dawn were the only people in his life that Jamie had met. He figured he had ages left until he had to mention the wedding to Jamie.

Sweat beaded on his forehead, and he wiped it with the hem of his T-shirt and hoped everyone would think it was because he was too warm. "Frank and Alice. I just thought it was a bit too soon to be talking weddings." It was almost true.

"I bet you've vlogged about him, am I right? How many thumbs up has he had?" Frank nudged him in the side. Liam shoved his hand away and sidestepped closer to Jamie.

Jamie's smile slipped, and he furrowed his brow in confusion. Liam didn't know what to say. Shit, he was bad at this stuff. He wasn't boyfriend material. He was great for a night, but anything more, and he'd screw it up. His life was in slow motion, and he knew it was going to end badly, so his mind raced to find something that would make it sound better, but the words had left him, and he careened face first into Shit Creek.

Dane and Markus were busy talking with Ben, who had just shown up. Only Paul kept glancing over at them. Anger started to simmer, and Liam wanted to go over there and thump him and then ask what he was staring at. But he knew it wasn't Paul's fault. He was just directing the anger he felt at himself at the one person he hated the most.

"Vlog?" Jamie asked. "I'm lost here."

Frank was oblivious to the tension, so drunk he was swaying. He laughed for no reason. Everything was a game to him as he rode high on booze. His filter was well and truly gone.

"He's like the Casanova of YouTube. It's hilarious. He goes on random dates with all these men." Frank knocked back the rest of his beer, and amber liquid trailed down his chin. Fuck, he was a mess. Alice was going to be so pissed off at him—but not as pissed off as Liam was.

"Really?" Jamie didn't sound angry. He wasn't upset or hurt. There seemed to be no emotion at all. Jamie didn't move, but Liam felt the distance stretch between them. Panic tightened his throat.

"It's not what you're thinking," he said desperately, reaching for something, anything.

"And just what am I thinking?"

Liam grimaced and swallowed. "I don't even know right now."

Frank finally stayed quiet and watched them both as the realisation of what he had said evidently dawned on him. "You should see the one where he lost his date at Zombie Brum City." Liam hadn't realised Frank had seen that one.

"Stop talking, Frankie. Just piss off." It was so busy the chatter of people made it difficult to concentrate.

"The escape room in Digbeth?" It looked like Jamie was putting two and two together. *Shit.* He was going to get the wrong idea.

Liam hesitated before touching Jamie's arm and frowned when he flinched. "Can we go somewhere quieter?"

Jamie allowed Liam to steer him to a quiet corner of the pub. Then he waited.

The tension between them was thick, the simmering anger palpable. "What can I say that won't make you mad?" he finally decided to say.

"What's your username?"

"L of a Ride," he admitted with a sigh. Liam bit at the skin on his bottom lip until he tasted blood.

Jamie laughed then and shook his head, eyes everywhere but on Liam. "And I'm in it?"

"Not technically, but I do talk about you. Not your name, but... yeah." He was making a real pig's ear of this. "I told you, I don't know what I'm doing. I've only ever had one boyfriend before, and that didn't last long. Even rebound boyfriends fuck up." He felt sick bringing that up, but he'd do anything to explain.

"Tell me." He said it so softly that Liam didn't hear him, but he hadn't lied when he told Jamie he could lip-read, so there was no getting out of it.

He told Jamie everything—Frank's negative plus-one, his idea to find someone to date long enough to change that, and how he'd used Jamie's pain to get his own way, becoming the perfect rebound.

An invisible wall stood between them. Jamie didn't cry, but his eyes were hard, his mouth pinched. He wasn't the laid-back musician, and he wasn't Mr Grumpy. He wasn't anything right then.

"The stupid thing is, Liam." *Liam*, not *Bowie*. "If you'd been honest with me from the start, I probably still would have taken you up on your offer. I was desperate enough to take what you had to offer so I didn't have to feel the pain again. Why didn't you just tell me everything?" He laughed, and the sound grated on Liam's ears. "I'm going home. Don't follow me."

# Chapter Eighteen

WHEN PAUL left him, Jamie cried. With Liam's revelation, he felt nothing. His eyes were dry. They felt like sandpaper when he blinked, and his chest felt hollow.

There was no point in being mad or hurt. So Liam hadn't given him the details, but he had let him know that he wasn't up for anything serious. Rebounds weren't meant to turn into anything more than what they were.

Jamie had forgotten. Liam was so easy to be around, and Jamie had needed someone after Paul and Tommy. The deceit shouldn't hurt, and it didn't, not really, not while he was still numb. Perhaps he'd stay that way.

He didn't want to look at Liam's videos, but he couldn't stop thinking about them either, twisting them in his mind until they were this huge monstrosity and Liam was a pantomime villain.

He opened the YouTube app on his phone. Liam was too easy to find. Jamie shook his head as he scrolled through, finger hesitating on one said *Rat Show—Find a Date*. He ran his tongue over his teeth, let out a breath, and steeled himself for it.

He pressed play and forced himself to watch. Jamie recognised that smile, the charming tone of voice and the cocky way he ran his hand through his hair. It was how he'd acted when they first met. Gradually that had disappeared, and he'd seen the real Liam. He wasn't too sure of that now. There were many faces of Liam, and he was brilliant at every single one.

Another video followed—a clip of him sitting in a toilet cubicle that was very familiar. The one Frank mentioned from the night they met. Was that what he was doing when he ran out of the double doors and crashed into him?

No wonder his date was chasing him. He cringed. Stark padded into the living room, meowed as she jumped onto him, and kneaded his lap with her paws until she settled down. He absently stroked her head with one hand, eyes not moving from his phone.

He remembered seeing Liam at the rat show and believing he was one of those popular types who only loved themselves. The videos described that version of him to a T.

The front door opened, and he wasn't surprised when Dane slipped onto the sofa next to him, still wearing his jacket. His hug was cold but more than welcome. Jamie's throat ached as he swallowed, and he just shook his head and leaned it against Dane's shoulder.

Dane pressed a kiss to his cheek. "Tell me all about it."

Jamie admitted that he was using Liam as a rebound to help him get over Paul, and Dane didn't seem too surprised. They talked and watched until Jamie couldn't take it anymore and switched his phone off.

"Well, in those last few videos," Dane started, "he seems to like you, darling."

Jamie shrugged, so tired that his eyelids kept drooping. He didn't know what to believe anymore. He just wanted to sleep for eternity.

"It shouldn't matter, should it? If he was just a guy I'm sleeping with to get over Paul?"

"If he was just a guy, no."

"Fucking Paul. If he hadn't run off with Tommy, this wouldn't have happened."

Dane stroked his hand through Jamie's hair, and he leaned into it like a cat. "True, but you'd be stuck with Paul." Dane gave a fake shudder, and Jamie laughed against his shoulder.

"Why didn't he just tell me?"

"I don't know, darling. We're men. Why do we do anything? I will say one thing—despite apparently dating you to get one over on his cousin, he talks about you an awful lot in those last few vlogs."

"What does that even mean?" It was slightly terrifying that the whole world knew about him and their relationship. He could walk by people in the street who had watched Liam talk about him. Could that be classed as stalking? He flashed back to Nightingale's and realised that had indeed happened, and he hadn't had a clue.

The doorbell rang, and he flinched. It could only be one person.

"Do you want to speak to him?" Dane asked.

The question was too difficult. Jamie didn't know what he wanted. No, that wasn't true. He just wanted life to be easy again. "I told him not to follow me." He glared toward the door but then sighed. "I suppose I'd better."

Dane pushed himself off the sofa. "I'll let him in and head home. Call if you need anything."

A few seconds later Liam filled the doorway to the living room. Blond hair messy as though he'd run his hands through it one too many times, his mouth strained, and his odd eyes tense. He licked his lips a few times. "I don't want to be your rebound."

Pain took Jamie's breath, and he found it hard to breathe. He preferred the numbness.

Liam stepped into the room. "I want us to be real. God… I don't even know how you feel." He shuffled, hands loose in his pockets. "Do you love Paul?"

Jamie jumped, confused at how the conversation was going. Where had that come from? "Paul? This isn't even about him. It's about you lying to me."

"I didn't expect to feel like this, all right? I spent years trying not to. It's easier not to feel anything."

Jamie could understand that.

"I had this boyfriend at university, took him home to meet the folks, then overheard him saying shit about Mom and Beth. I was so fucking… hurt." Liam gave a bitter laugh. "Then you came along, and I kept bumping into you, literally. I thought you'd be the perfect person to take to Frank's wedding, and you are. Only I don't want it to be fake."

What was he saying? Jamie's heart pounded. "I don't know what you're saying."

"Do you still love Paul?"

Jamie thought about it, poked at the cracks in his heart, and realised it didn't hurt quite so badly. It was tender, fragile, but Liam had put it back together, piece by piece, without either of them realising.

"I did once. Not anymore."

Liam let out a relieved breath. "I'm emotionally delayed. The most serious relationship I've ever had is this one. But Jamie, I don't want to be your rebound boyfriend. I want to be your *boyfriend*."

Liam stepped toward the sofa and looked down at him. Jamie couldn't seem to make his limbs work. His heart hammered in his chest and his mouth became dry.

"I'm sorry I never told you about the vlog or the wedding."

"I think I'd like that." Jamie licked his lips. Liam dropped to his knees in front of him and clutched Jamie's knees.

"Like what?"

"To be your boyfriend." He was feeling shock, but underneath it, a kernel of joy grew until his chest swelled.

Jamie's lips trembled as he leaned forward and captured Liam's lips in a tender kiss. At first it was a gentle brush of the lips, but it gradually got deeper until Jamie caved and pushed his tongue into Liam's mouth, reacquainting himself with the taste and feel that was so uniquely Liam.

# Chapter Nineteen

SINCE THEY officially became boyfriends, sans rebound, they took the time to learn more about each other, learning quirks, likes, and dislikes. Liam was petrified of spiders, but Jamie loved them.

Jamie collected Marvel figures, and Liam liked to put them in obscene positions and wait to see if Jamie would notice. He always did.

Agatha had a litter of beautiful Russian Blue rats Liam had fallen in love with. He'd be heartbroken when they went to their new homes, but he would soon get distracted by the next litter.

Jamie's favourite activity was going for walks over the heathland he maintained, to see the plant life and animals he'd helped to thrive. He couldn't stop smiling as he showed Liam around and pointed out various things to him. Liam seemed genuinely interested and he let Jamie babble on without getting irritated or looking bored.

"Where is it we're going?" Liam asked as they walked hand in hand over Chasewater Dam.

"I'm taking you on a date I can guarantee you've not been on before." Jamie looked sideways at him and raised an eyebrow. "It'll be vlog-worthy," he teased. Liam groaned and swung their hands faster.

They'd taken an afternoon stroll around the reservoir, walking up over the dam so they could watch birds fly over the dappled expanse and waterskiers make fools of themselves in the distance.

Jamie pointed out three black-and-white Oystercatchers all standing on one leg in a line along the pier. They stopped so Liam could look properly, guarding his eyes against the sun and following Jamie's finger.

Liam might not be a nature expert, but there was no denying his enthusiasm. The pier was closed off to the public and had been for as long as Jamie could remember, although that hadn't stopped him or his friends sneaking over the barriers when they were teenagers to drink White Lightning. It was a wonder none of them had fallen in and drowned.

The dam curved down toward the South Shore Café, and they stopped to buy a bottle of water and share it as they carried on.

Jamie knew most of the staff who worked there, from those who worked in the café and Innovation Centre to those who manned the boating pond. It took them longer as they stopped to talk to people, but Liam went with the flow, not frustrated or angry.

They wound their way around the ruins of the small stone castle on the edge of the water and down through the shrubs. Jamie knew this land better than anyone and he took them off the main pathways and away from the tourists and walkers.

"Heathland is rarer than the rainforest. See that plant over there? It's carnivorous and eats insects." Jamie was babbling, but he loved talking about this, and Liam was an avid student.

"What's it called?" Liam pulled him over to peer closely at it and watch it trap flies in its dewy leaves.

"It's a sundew. See how it wraps its leaves around the flies?" They watched it for a few moments more before carrying on. They stepped carefully through the heathers and gorse, a blanket of purple flowers and lush green grasses underfoot.

"I had no idea there were so many cool plants over here. I just thought it was wasteland. I had no clue you have to do so much work to make sure everything thrives."

"There are so many rare species of animals, plants, and birds here. We have to maintain the heath so the habitat is correct for them. It's pretty interesting. If you're into this type of thing." Jamie felt his cheeks start to burn. He'd bored Paul to death. Even his family zoned out when he talked too much about the local wildlife. He hoped he wasn't boring the hell out of Liam. He chanced a look in his direction, but Liam was looking around with genuine interest, so he relaxed and made an effort to just enjoy the day.

Jamie wasn't the avid bird spotter—that was Tommy—but he enjoyed a walk in the countryside and hearing the birds sing. He knew many different varieties from sight or song, but his true passion was the heathland and the wildlife that lived there.

Showing this to Liam made his heart swell with happiness. He squeezed Liam's hand as they carried on walking, and Liam looked at him and smiled, his eyes bright and his nose a little sunburned.

It usually only took an hour and a half to walk around the reservoir, but they meandered and walked off the beaten track. By the time they made it to the country roads that would lead them to where they would spend their evening, it had started to get dark.

He navigated them toward a large country house, too grand to be called a farmhouse but not quite an estate. Veering off the large manicured garden into a copse of gnarled trees, they followed a slight trail in the shrub that led to a clearing and a cluster of barns. Two were renovated while the third looked beaten and weather worn.

There was a blanket and a wicker picnic basket set up on the grass in front of the barns.

"What's this?" Liam said, sounding pleased.

"I know the woman who owns this house—Lady Sarah Pinfield. She helped with the picnic and gave us permission to use the gardens." He'd met her through work, and despite their obvious class differences, they got along like a house on fire. He pulled Liam over to the picnic, sat down, and opened the basket.

"Oh, posh," Liam said as Jamie started to investigate.

He should have known that leaving the food to Sarah would mean fewer sausage rolls and Walkers crisps and more potato salad and stinky cheese. The bottle of Lambrini he'd asked for was replaced by a bottle of champagne he knew must have cost a bomb. He was going to have to have words with her when he spoke to her next.

Jamie leaned back on his elbows and nodded toward the barn. "See that barn? It doesn't look much. You might wonder why the rest of the house and gardens are in such great condition, but that still looks like it did fifty years ago. There's a bat roost there. Each night at dusk, they leave the roost to hunt."

"What do they hunt? Do they suck the blood of humans?" Liam leaned over and sucked at Jamie's neck, making him laugh and push him away. Then Liam opened the champagne and poured some into two glasses—Jamie noticed they were crystal, not plastic.

"They suck the blood out of insects. I think you'll be safe with me." Jamie winked and settled down to eat. "I thought we could watch them, maybe listen to them."

"We're going to watch bats? Bats are cool. They look like rats with dragon wings."

"They get around with sonar, but if we use this handy device, we can actually hear them." From his rucksack he pulled out a bat detector that looked a like a walkie talkie. "As part of our job, we have to check out bat roosts because they're protected. Sarah contacted us a few years ago to tell us about this roost, so we come and count the bats every now and then."

"You count them?"

"Yep. Don't worry. We just get to watch them tonight. Sarah's become an avid bat advocate since discovering this roost. She wanted to convert this building too, but now she's leaving it for them."

"That's actually really nice."

"She is nice—very posh, *naughty*," he said, thinking of the champagne, "but lovely."

"So when do we get to see them? Can I hold one?" He smiled, and his whole face lit up like it did when he held the rats.

"No holding unless you have a license, but they're very interesting to watch." Jamie turned the detector and fiddled with the frequency until it was right.

They finished off the food and pushed the basket away so they could lie on their backs side by side. The moon was bright, and stars were just starting to twinkle as darkness fell.

It was still warm enough that they only needed light jackets, and Jamie could feel Liam's body heat at his side. He placed an arm casually over Liam's stomach and leaned his head against his shoulder.

There were other roosts he could have taken him to, but Jamie knew this one would give them privacy, and it was such a beautiful location that he wanted to share it with Liam.

"They should come out right over there." Jamie pointed to the top right-hand corner of the barn, and they both watched and waited, neither in a hurry to fill the silence—though it wasn't silent at all. The trees rustled in the light breeze, insects buzzed, and an owl hooted in the distance. There was so much life it was truly breathtaking.

As they waited for the bats, Jamie heard a noise that was part way between a frog and a cricket, only more lyrical. He tensed against Liam, breath caught in his throat as he scanned the darkening sky.

"What?" Liam whispered.

He didn't say anything at first, just kept searching. Then he spotted it—just a blur between the trees and the side of the barn. Jamie pointed toward it, and Liam strained to look. "There."

"Is it a bat?" Jamie could hear the confusion in Liam's voice. He shook his head.

"No, it's a nightjar. They're nocturnal birds, and they're hard to spot. I've never seen one before." He gave a breathy laugh and tightened his arms around Liam. "You're obviously my lucky charm." It landed in the tree and was obscured by the branches, though they could still hear it.

"I am full of marshmallowy goodness," he agreed. They drifted back into silence so they could listen to the lyrical churring until it flew away. It was probably there less than a minute, but Jamie couldn't help but think of it as a good omen for them and their relationship. He'd never seen one with Paul, after all.

"Wow." Jamie didn't even try to contain his excitement. "In folklore it's believed they stole milk from goats."

"How is that even possible?"

"I'm not really sure. They were always found near livestock. They got the name goat sucker." They were both chuckling when a whooshing noise interrupted them. They looked back toward the barn and, seconds later, Jamie saw a dark blur.

"Look," he whispered needlessly.

The bats darted from the hole beneath the roof and danced in the darkness above their heads, barely visible. They didn't fly smoothly like birds but darted around in fast, jagged movements, their black wings creating dappled shadows in the moonlight.

"Look at that," Liam said, his voice full of wonder. "I've seen the odd bat before, but never anything like this." The bat detector whirred to life with high-pitched whistles chattering over each other. "Is that the bats?"

Jamie nodded, enjoying Liam's reaction more than watching the bats. Paul had never been an outdoor person, and he could take or leave animals. Jamie wouldn't even contemplate doing something like this with him, but he wanted to share it with Liam.

Jamie rolled into Liam's side and placed his head back on Liam's shoulder. "They're called pipistrelles. They're the most common here, and they're tiny little fluff balls."

They watched the bats until every last one left the roost and flew off to fill up on insects. The bat detector quietened, and Jamie turned it off.

"That thing is amazing. I can't believe we got to hear bats."

"It's even more amazing than that. You can actually hear rats chatter on it."

"What? No way?"

"It's very cute. We'll have a go when we get home."

"That is truly amazing. I can talk to the girls! I enjoyed this. Thank you." Liam kissed him, hard and brief, with just the trail of tongue on his lips as he pulled away.

Jamie licked his lips, tasted Liam's unique flavour, and wanted more. Soon. "It's not over yet. See that barn over there?" He pointed to one on the right. "It's been converted into a cottage. Sarah said we could have it for the night."

Liam's eyebrows rose toward his forehead. "I've not brought any clean clothes with me." His voice was liquid gold with a hint of gravel, which made goosebumps appear on Jamie's arms.

"You won't need them," Jamie promised.

# Chapter Twenty

Car Maintenance for Aliens
  *L_ofa_Ride*
  6 years ago. 983K Views

Liam yawned and his jaw clicked as he stared at the screen. Catching up on his social media was a mammoth task. He'd neglected his channel since he officially got together with Jamie, not because Jamie didn't approve—he liked some of his videos—but because he was too busy. He'd finally found something, or someone, more important than his vlog.

And therein lay the problem. He didn't need to vlog about dating because he'd already found the perfect guy.

He watched some of his very first videos and cringed at how young he looked, how awful his editing was, and what on earth he'd been wearing. The one thing that jumped out, apart from all that, was that he had something to teach someone. There was a purpose.

He'd always loved cars—not fast, expensive ones, but rather the sense of freedom that came from them. He loved road trips and tinkering under the bonnet with his dad. When he passed his test at seventeen, he was surprised how many people didn't know the basics about car maintenance. That thought stuck with him all the way to university, where he was one of the few students who had his license.

The first-ever video he filmed was beyond basics. *Car Maintenance for Aliens*, he'd called it, and he explained the headlights, the gears, how to fill up at a petrol station. His lecturers had scoffed at the content, but hundreds of people watched it that first week. Even now he had comments.

He did a few others like that before the channel took a turn into what it was now. Ironically, if he'd carried on how he was, it might have helped more when he decided to become a driving instructor.

There was one video he'd made but never posted it because it wasn't what his viewers watched him for, and he didn't want to be ridiculed. It was safer for his ego to carry on producing what people wanted.

It wasn't a bad video, but there was something missing…. He stared at the screen until he was cross-eyed.

Jamie opened the door wearing only his boxer shorts. His cheek had pillow creases, and his hair stuck out in every direction. Rubbing his eyes with the heel of his hand, he draped himself over the back of Liam's chair and made it swing sideways gently.

"What you doin'?" His words were still sleepy as he peered over Liam's shoulder toward the screen.

Liam pressed a kiss to his arm and stared at the screen again. "Just trying to figure out my channel."

Jamie tightened his arms around Liam's neck and rubbed his nose against Liam's hair. "You'll figure it out. Come to bed soon?"

Liam lifted his head, and they kissed awkwardly. "I will. Now go back to bed. It's late and you have work in the morning. Whereas I don't have to be up until midday."

Jamie laughed. "Yes, Dad. Though I might wake you up before I go to work."

Liam pouted and fluttered his eyelashes, his eyes darkening when Jamie edged the waistband of his boxers down over his hips. He knew how much Liam loved his hip bones. Jamie gave a breathy laugh and slipped out of the room. It took Liam a while before he could concentrate on the screen again.

The idea sprang to him when he found himself signing along to his videos, and he scrambled for his camera and attached it to the tripod. He switched on his lights, knowing the quality wouldn't be great but not wanting to wait to get his idea on film.

He watched his old video on his computer, turned the camera on, and aimed at his hands. He signed through everything he said on the screen and messed up a few times, but he could easily edit that out. Then he uploaded the new video to his computer.

When he finished, the video had a small box inlaid in the bottom right-hand corner with his hands signing along. It was rough, but he had a good feeling about it. Though it might not cater to the people who watched his dating videos, it would hopefully gain him new followers.

Before he thought too much about it, he uploaded it. Then he went to join Jamie in bed, snuggled into his side, and pulled the covers over them.

Jamie did indeed wake him up early the next morning.

Worth it.

# Chapter Twenty-One

SINCE LIAM had found out about the bat detector, he was obsessed with hearing the rats talk. They were in Jamie's living room, and Mabel, Gert, and Maud were running over the sofa while he tried to get them to stand on their back legs by dangling treats above their heads.

"Up," he told them, and they all started to push each other away so they could be the one to grab hold of the yoghurt drop and run off. He wasn't having a huge success, but the girls were having fun. Liam heard the distinct chatter through the bat detector.

"I think I'm starting to understand them."

Jamie burst out laughing and tickled Mabel's ears. "What are they saying?"

"Mabel is enjoying being stroked. Maud is telling me if she's expected to do tricks, she wants more than yoghurt drops. Gert just wants all the yoghurt drops."

"You're adorable. They sound like very intelligent rats. Come on. Dinner should be ready. You put the girls back, and I'll plate up." Jamie patted his stomach and pushed himself off the sofa.

"Need help?"

Jamie shook his head. "You sort the girls, then find us something ridiculous to watch." Jamie walked into the kitchen and plated up the spaghetti Bolognese. He wasn't much of a cook, but he had the basics covered.

They rarely dined at the kitchen table, preferring to sit and watch trashy TV while they ate. Jamie carried their plates in and put Liam's on the coffee table in the middle of the room. He'd already put in a DVD for them.

"Good choice. I've not seen that in ages," he said when Liam came back from putting the rats away.

"*Attack of the Killer Tomatoes!* is suitably trashy, I thought. Thank you for dinner. You didn't have to. We could have ordered a Chinese."

"I don't mind." Jamie got his own plate, and they settled onto the sofa to watch the credits. Stark appeared out of nowhere and jumped up to sit between them, making them move outward to give her a little more room.

When they'd both eaten and their plates were empty on the floor, Jamie moved the cat and put her on Liam's lap so they could sit closer together.

"I love being boring with you," Jamie said.

"Well, I'm glad I'm boring." Liam winked at him and flicked his arm. Jamie rolled his eyes, but the affectionate flick kept the smile on his face.

They'd both slid down the sofa and were lying tangled together, napping more than paying any attention to the TV, with Stark lying on their feet, when Jamie heard the key turn in the lock. He frowned and twisted his head around, wondering why Dane felt the need to use his key.

"Only me," his mother called out. Jamie flinched. Guilt and embarrassment settled in his stomach, and he was frantically wondering where they could hide when she pushed the door open.

"Oh shit." He didn't know what else to say. This was not how he wanted Liam to meet his mother, and it was not how he wanted to introduce Liam to her. He was a bad, bad son for putting it off for so long. He hadn't even told her about Liam yet because he wanted Liam to himself for just a little bit longer.

"There you boys are. I thought you'd been hiding from me. It's been months. I see your sister more, and she's away every other week on business, so I don't know what your excuse is. I decided to come and see if you were alive. I was sure you'd been eaten by that cat.... Hi, Paul—" ended on a high note when she realised it wasn't Paul on the sofa with him.

*Oh shit. Fuck.* He'd been avoiding the conversation because she always made a mountain out of a molehill.

"He's not Paul." She glared at them, mouth pursed tightly.

"No, he's not. I'm sure I told you about Liam? I left a message on Dad's mobile." It was a poor lie, and they both knew it.

She scoffed. "Your father? You know he doesn't use that thing. It's easier leaving a message for Prince Harry than your father. What do I keep telling you?" *Don't lie about leaving messages for his dad?*

Jamie climbed off the sofa and walked over to her, desperately wondering how to defuse the situation. "I told you that key was for emergencies." He gave a nervous laugh.

"Well, when my son doesn't visit for months, it is an emergency. What are you doing with another man? Where is Paul?" She crossed her arms and looked down her nose at him, which was a feat in itself as he was taller than her.

Liam gave him a disappointed look, as if to ask why he hadn't told her yet. Jamie knew Liam spoke to his parents every week and visited almost as much. He hadn't met them yet, but it was only a matter of time. "You could have knocked on the door instead of letting yourself in. Paul's probably at Tommy's." Saying the words didn't hurt like they used to.

"Tommy's? Why would he be there? What did you do?" She glared at Liam as though it were his fault, twisting her key between her fingers.

"What did we do? They've been having an affair," he bit out, finally admitting it. He felt guilty for not talking to his mom about it, but she had a habit of making things seem so much worse.

She gasped and covered her mouth with her hands. "Paul and Tommy?"

This was not a conversation he wanted in front of Liam. How awkward. He didn't want him to know how much it still bothered him. Not that he wanted Paul back, but the betrayal still hurt, and he didn't like to admit to his mom that he'd failed at something. It was irrational because he knew she'd be on his side when she had all the facts. "It's true. He admitted it at the rat show a while back," he said.

"At the rat show? Who would split up with someone like that?" She sounded indignant. "I think I need to give them boys a piece of my mind," she said. He had a horrible thought that she'd storm around to Tommy's and rip them to shreds. He winced at the image, though a part of him wanted to see what she'd do. His mom was fierce.

"You don't need to bother about them anymore. I'm over it. This is Liam, my new boyfriend. Liam, this is Maureen, my mom."

Liam stood and held his hand out to her. Unfortunately he was wearing one of his *L*

*of a Ride* T-shirts, so she probably thought he'd hired an escort. "It's a pleasure to meet you, Maureen."

"You too, even if it is a bit of a shock. I hope you're going to be a better boyfriend than Paul." She shook Liam's hand and didn't let go. "Did I tell you I've already knitted Paul Christmas socks?" She shook Liam's hand but looked at Jamie.

"Send them to Tommy's." Jamie swallowed his irritation. Why did she even care? They were socks.

She squeezed Liam's hand tighter, and he yelped a little. "Over my dead body. He hurt my boy. I'm not sending him anything." She pulled on Liam until he stooped down to her. "Do you like socks, Liam?"

"I adore socks. I wear them every day." He wiggled his toes for her, and she nodded.

Satisfied, she let go of him, and Jamie had to bite the inside of his cheek to stop from laughing as Liam massaged life back into his hand.

"Mom knits socks for us all at Christmas," Jamie explained.

"Like Mrs Weasley, but with socks, not jumpers," Liam said. Jamie did laugh then. It was an accurate image.

"I'll have you know I can knit better than she can, and I don't have magic. Are you going to offer me a cup of tea, Jamie, or am I going to die of thirst?" She arched one eyebrow at him as she made herself comfortable on the sofa. She patted the spot next to her. "Come on, Liam. Tell me all about how you met my son. Considering he's not told me anything, it's up to you to fill me in."

She shot Jamie a glare, and he fled to the kitchen, happy to make tea and escape for a little while.

"I don't believe it," he heard her say from the kitchen. Oh God, what was Liam telling her? He should never have left them alone. "Will you be spending Christmas with Jamie? You're more than welcome to come to us."

"It's not even autumn yet. Stop talking about Christmas," Jamie shouted.

"Shut up, you, and make my tea," she shouted back but with a smile in her voice.

His heart galloped at the thought of Christmas, or spending Christmas with Liam. Not because he didn't want it, because he did, but because it was so far in the future, and it was still weird to think he wouldn't be spending the holidays with Paul.

He made the tea, carried it through to the living room, and set the cups down on the coffee table.

"About time. You'd think he'd been dragged up." She patted Jamie on the arm and winked at Liam, taking the sting out of her words. Was Jamie in some alternate universe or something? How had Liam won her over so easily? It was official. Liam had to be there whenever he talked to her about anything.

They chatted for a while longer. She cursed Paul's name and vowed never to let Tommy into her house again. Then she left them to it, but only after they promised to come around for dinner soon.

"She's an experience." Liam seemed a little dazed, and Jamie didn't blame him. She was his mother, and he felt the same.

"She is. Sorry about that. She's a bit intense, and as much as I love her, she's best received in small doses. I don't know what you said to her. She's never warmed to someone so fast."

"I charmed her, of course. You need to visit your parents more," Liam scolded him, but there was no bite to his words, and Jamie relaxed and dropped his head to Liam's shoulder.

"Don't get me wrong, I love her. I adore her. But she's overwhelming."

"Don't worry. Mothers, and women in general, all love me. It's my superpower," Liam said somewhat smugly.

"I wouldn't call that your superpower…." Jamie lifted his head and gazed at him, hoping the heat in his eyes would distract him from the conversation. He loved how Liam looked lounging against the sofa. He didn't even have to try to be sexy. He just *was*. And Jamie really didn't want to talk about his mother anymore.

"Oh really?" Liam licked his lips, and Jamie's cock started to harden.

Jamie stood and pulled his T-shirt over his head and watched Liam's eyes darken and his nostrils flare as he took in Jamie's bare skin. "Really." Jamie's voice was low and full of promise. Liam pushed himself up from the sofa, grabbed the hem of his own T-shirt, and yanked it over his head as he stood in front of Jamie.

Jamie cupped Liam's jaw and guided their mouths together in a deep, wet kiss.

MEETING JAMIE'S mom, while it had been an experience, made Liam think he should introduce Jamie to his parents. They were dying to meet him, but he'd been waiting for Jamie to let him know when it was socially acceptable to meet the parents. He had no clue when the right time was, and out of all the weird and wonderful things that came with a new relationship, meeting the parents scared him the most.

Richard—his one and only boyfriend before Jamie—had broken down when he met Liam's family. Liam always thought it hadn't bothered him. Only now that he was in a serious relationship did he realise how it had affected him, down to making a mockery of it on his vlog. Rationally he knew Jamie would have no issues with his family being deaf, but he couldn't stop the tendril of fear taking root.

"Are we at the 'meet the parents stage' yet or not?" He asked the question lightly, not giving away the seriousness of his thoughts.

Jamie was lying on the living room floor reading a book. He looked over the pages at him. "I have no idea. I'm used to a mother who takes those kind of choices away." He smiled and rolled his eyes, then dog-eared the page of his book and pushed himself up to sit cross-legged. "Don't get me wrong, my mother is amazing. Neither of my parents ever had any issues when I came out, and she's always been as invested in my boyfriends as she has my sister's. She's just full on."

"My folks were good about it too. I mean, my dad was shocked but not upset or anything like that." He'd bonded with Selena at school and never felt like he had to hide who he was. "I liked your mom. She's funny. Once she gave me the third degree about not hurting her wildly successful and talented son, she asked for my shoe size so she could knit me socks." Liam presumed that was his initiation into the family. He quite liked it. Maureen was one part sweet eccentric lady and one part lioness protecting her child. Castration may have been mentioned if he ever hurt Jamie, but Liam thought it best not to mention that. He felt a little sorry for her that Jamie actively seemed to avoid her, and didn't want to make it worse.

Jamie groaned and faceplanted into his hands. "She's so embarrassing. And loud and an aggressive knitter."

Liam smirked at him and poked Jamie's knee with his toe. "She even showed me the photo of you she carries around in her purse." He loved seeing tiny Jamie looking all awkward and cute.

Jamie's eyes widened, and he looked up from between his fingers. "Oh God, she did not."

"She did. You were adorable dressed as Joseph in the school nativity with your neon knitted headdress."

"One day I'm going to find the original photo and burn it so she can't make more copies. What mother knits them a neon green-and-yellow headdress with a bright pink band for a nativity play?"

"Poor Jamie. She loves you so, so much. I feel your pain." Liam laughed. "She loves you *so* much she spent hours working her fingers to the bone to make sure you had the best costumes a boy could want. You should feel guilty for not appreciating her more," he teased.

"No child would want that costume. It itched like crazy, and I looked like Joseph if he'd been on acid. Did she tell you that on my twenty-first birthday she blew up copies of that photo and put them all around town? Everyone saw it. My doctor, my boss, my friends. The blokes at the pub. Tommy helped her put them up. They ribbed me about it for months."

Liam laughed but didn't react at the mention of Tommy. He didn't want Jamie to think he couldn't mention him, and if he was talking about him without getting upset, hopefully that meant he was getting over it.

"She didn't tell me that. I would have loved to see your face. I bet you were so serious at twenty-one, pretending to be cool so you could get all the boys." Liam slipped off the sofa and sat opposite him on the floor.

"Stop laughing," Jamie said, but Liam could see his lips twitching as well. "I was very cool at twenty-one. I'm actually even cooler now."

Liam attempted to keep his face straight, but he snorted and another laugh escaped. "I don't think you're cool," Liam said. In fact he thought Jamie was hot—very hot. His eyes travelled down Jamie's body. His worn T-shirt accentuated his hard chest, and his jeans were threadbare in the most delicious of places. Liam forgot how to breathe as he watched Jamie's eyes darken under his gaze.

Liam shuffled closer to him, and with a firm hand, pushed Jamie onto his back and crawled over him. Their bodies fit together like they were made for each other. It didn't matter what they were doing. Sitting next to each other, holding each other, sex, just being in the same room... they fit. He never thought he'd ever find that kind of connection, and despite not wanting it to begin with, he was glad he had it.

Jamie groaned and ran his hands up the back of Liam's T-shirt, sending shivers down his spine. "What were we talking about, again?" Jamie asked.

Liam couldn't think about anything else with Jamie beneath him, and when Jamie lifted his head and offered Liam his lips, he couldn't resist tasting him. His eyes fluttered closed and he concentrated on the feel of Jamie's tongue against his. Liam kept the kiss slow and light, even when Jamie thrust against him, trying to up the tempo.

When Liam pulled away Jamie licked his lips to lure him back. It almost worked, but they were having an important conversation. Jamie wasn't the only one to forget what they'd been talking about. It took him a good thirty seconds before he remembered. "We were talking about meeting the family."

It took Jamie a few moments to catch up. "Oh. I remember. You'd like my dad. He's as quiet as Mom is loud. I'd like to meet your parents and sister, too. They can't be as bad as Frank."

Liam groaned and shook his head. Bloody Frank and his huge feet. He didn't know what Alice saw in him sometimes. "No one is as bad as Frank. But we could go around one evening after work… if you wanted."

Jamie sent him a warm glance and rolled him over so they both lay side by side in front of the fireplace. "I want to."

"My mom's deaf, just so you know. My sister is too. They both lip-read, though, so you'll be fine." He pushed the words out quickly, and Jamie looked at him again and tightened his grip around his waist.

"I wondered why you knew sign language." Surprise must have shown on his face, because Jamie laughed. "You move your hands subconsciously when you speak sometimes, and one of the first things you told me was that you could lip-read."

He hadn't realised he still did that. He'd tried to stop it when he started school and the other kids would pick on him for it.

"Perhaps you could teach me some sign language," Jamie said. Liam liked the sound of that.

"Did I ever mention to you that I'm deaf in my left ear too?"

Jamie pulled back to stare at him, mouth dropping open. "No. Well, that explains a few things." Jamie pressed a kiss to his jawline.

"Like what?"

"Like when I whisper dirty things into your left ear when we're in bed, you don't always respond."

Liam's jeans suddenly felt tight. "Really? What saucy things did I miss? We need to try that again, and you can whisper sweet nothings into my right ear."

Jamie licked a trail up to his ear and sucked the lobe into his mouth. Then he let go and stood up. He held out his hand and pulled Liam to his feet. "We can start now, but I assure you, they won't be sweet *nothings*."

IT WAS much later that night when Liam got to hear every not-so-sweet nothing until they were too worn out to do anything but lie in bed and wait for sleep to take them. Was it too soon for this level of comfort? If it was, it still felt right.

"You have very talented fingers," Liam said, sated, voice quiet.

"Like my ukulele playing, huh?"

"I love your ukulele playing." He gave a feeble thrust of hips against Jamie's, but neither of them tried to take it further. "Why do you all play the ukulele and not a real guitar?"

Jamie pinched his arm. "Don't let Markus hear you call it that. It's a completely different instrument," Jamie said, mimicking Markus, using an awful Black Country accent.

"When did you learn?"

Jamie absently trailed his hand back and forth across the back of Liam's neck. "My sister was given one as a Christmas present when we were kids, and I thought it was a guitar and kind of stole it from her. I wouldn't leave it alone, and eventually my folks got me a book, and when I badgered them again, I got lessons. I gave it up when I became a teenager because ukuleles are so not cool." He lifted his head to look at Liam and wiggled his eyebrows, which made him laugh. "But by the time university came around, all those uncool things became cool again, and one night the three of us decided we were going to start a band."

"After one too many beers, right?"

"Oh yeah. Dane already knew the basics, and Markus is some kind of mad genius, so we just started to jam and got good. Well, kind of."

"You *are* good."

Jamie pressed a kiss to the closest bit of bare flesh he could reach. "Thank you. Plus. Ukuleles are hilarious. Grown men playing rock on mini guitars just made us laugh. We stopped after university because Dane went on to study veterinary medicine and then got a job in a practice in the East Midlands. But we started again when he moved over this way, and we just got lucky, I guess. We've played a few different bars, even a wedding, but the Drunken Duck asks us to play all the time, so we can't be that bad. Either that or they know we're cheap and they can buy us with beer. Ukuleles *are* very manly. I've got *groupies*."

Liam burst out laughing, and Jamie's head shook with the movements of his chest. "I think *I'm* your groupie," Liam said. Then he leaned over and kissed him.

# Chapter Twenty-Two

MIRROR, SIGNAL, Manoeuvre
*L_ofa_Ride*
3 days ago. 52K Views

Once that first car maintenance video went up with added British Sign Language, life got busy. His content changed and he lost subscribers, but he gained others. He added Raturday Saturday, in which he waxed poetic about Mabel, Maud, and Gert. He spent a lot of time on different videos related to learning to drive, all of which he added BSL to. His sister loved them, his mom was stupidly proud, and his dad said he always knew he'd do something great eventually.

Jamie's bookcase became a backdrop to quite a few of his videos when he wasn't outside with the car or inside the car, but Jamie was adamant that he didn't want to be in them. He'd blush and stammer whenever Liam tried.

His rats lived in Jamie's spare cage whenever he stopped over, and Jamie and Liam went over to his parents' every other week—usually to be fed, because Jamie had fallen in love with his dad's homemade chips. He said it was a good job he was on the move all day or he'd be the size of a house.

As Liam had predicted, Jamie's mom loved him more and more each time they visited. His dad was quiet, but they both bonded over the Grand Prix, so they got along well. Even Jamie relaxed without the not-so-gentle complaints about his lack of visits and enjoyed the time he spent with his parents more.

Summer slowly turned into autumn, and driving lessons eased up as the weather became cold. Even so, his business was doing well, and companies started to send him things to review. Car wax, air fresheners—you name it, and he probably had it in his coat cupboard.

He was bringing in more money with ads and affiliates than he did with his previous videos, and although he still got the odd negative comment or DM from those people, it wasn't enough for him to stop the direction he was going in.

When Liam dropped off his last student on Saturday evening, he would head over to Jamie's. He didn't need the thrill of random hookups and weird dates anymore. He was content. He didn't even miss vlogging about it, which surprised him.

He had a better social life now. They went to clubs, danced until they were sweaty and found a dark corner to get off, and Jamie even went with him to the lesbian book club at the library. It was hard to find the time for everything, but Liam found he wanted to, and that was the biggest difference.

"They are so cute. How can you give them up?" Liam asked as he peered into the cage of one of Jamie's newest litters. Apparently they would be a mixture of Russian Blue and Russian Agouti. Jamie seemed very excited about them, but to Liam, they were just adorable babies.

Agatha had nine kittens, and although it was too early for Jamie to decide which ones he would be keeping and which would be offered to the people on his waiting list, Liam secretly thought boyfriend privileges should mean he got to keep them all. His heart was going to break when they went to their new homes.

"It's hard, but you get used to it. And I always keep at least two from each litter. They only ever go to pet homes unless I agree they can be bred, and I get first refusal if they ever have to be given up by their owners."

Jamie tried to talk to Liam about genetics and lines and lots of other complicated stuff, but Liam's knowledge went as far as "Aww, rat babies" and no further. As much as he adored rats, especially his three wonderful girls, he would leave the complicated stuff to Jamie.

The kittens wriggled in their basket of warm fleece in his lap. Jamie was cleaning out their cage and giving Agatha some extra love, which meant Liam got to hold the babies and photograph them, because every breath they took was just too precious. He'd even started to sing

"Every Breath You Take" to them, but Jamie had something against the Police and pleaded with him to stop.

As he took photos of them, a notification popped up on his phone—MC Glamour Time, real name Michael, a lifestyle YouTuber he'd known for years.

"Shit, I totally forgot about that." Every year a bunch of them tried to get together in real life and catch up. With Jamie, his vlog, and work, it had completely slipped his mind.

"What's that?" Jamie looked up from scrubbing the cage.

"Every year some of the vloggers try and meet up."

"That sounds interesting…." Jamie sounded a bit guarded, and Liam didn't blame him.

"It's nothing wild. Loads of us started vlogging around the same time and got to know each other online. MC—Mike—vlogs about makeup and hair, Amber vlogs about planners and bullet journals…. Lots of different types of channels. We usually go for a weekend, drink too much coffee in the day, too many cocktails in the evenings, and then head home and vlog about it." Liam really wasn't sure if he should invite Jamie to go with him or ask permission to go. "What do you think? Should I go?"

"Bowie, if you want to go, you should. You don't need to worry about me. I trust you." Jamie sauntered over and pressed a quick kiss to his lips, sucking his bottom lip between his teeth. It made Liam shudder and did exactly as Jamie intended it. He took the rat basket out of his lap and put them back into the cage with their momma. "I'm not going to demand that you don't go or say you have to take me with you." Rats back in the cage, Jamie sat down on Liam's lap and draped his arms around Liam's neck.

Liam hugged him, loving the weight of him. "I'm new at this boyfriend lark. I don't know what's right or wrong, as we've already found out."

Jamie rolled his eyes and then pulled his earlobe. "Silly man. Anyway, someone needs to stay home and watch the kids." He nodded toward the rats. "You can bring your rats here while you're away."

"Thank you." Liam twisted around on the chair, making Jamie hold on to him tighter. Liam pushed the heel of his foot against the floor, twisted them around even faster, and Jamie let out a curse but didn't move from his lap. They kissed, clashing tongues as the chair carried on spinning. Liam was dizzy, but he couldn't tell if it was from the chair or Jamie's kisses.

Jamie pulled back, lips glistening. "I reek of rat. Want to shower?" He wiggled his eyebrows, and Liam made sure he had a good hold of him, stood up, and half carried, half dragged him to the bathroom.

Jamie had one of those old ornate-looking bathtubs with the clawed feet. It was much too deep to climb inside without dropping Jamie and cracking his skull open on the ceramic, so Liam put Jamie on his feet and let him turn on the shower while he got undressed.

When they were both naked, they stepped under the steaming-hot spray, and the shower curtain closed them off to the rest of the world until it was just the two of them. No exes, no friends, no awkward parents—just them. Jamie reached for the shower gel, but Liam took it from him, squirted it into his hands, lathered it up, and slowly soaped each of Jamie's work-roughened fingers.

He washed him all over, slipping his hands over his quivering belly, the sharp lines of his hips, and the hot tension of his erection. Jamie groaned and closed his eyes as water ran down his face and plastered his hair to his skull. He looked so exposed standing there under the spray without the mop of curly hair to hide behind.

Liam's heart thumped, desire charged each touch, and his fingers tingled. He dropped to his knees and pressed his cheek against Jamie's erection. Then he slowly sucked it into his mouth, making Jamie's knees almost buckle.

Jamie's cock was long and slick and slid to the back of Liam's throat as though it were made to be there. He tasted of shower gel with just a hint of salt before the water washed it away. Liam tensed his tongue, and as he drew back, licked a line on the underside.

Jamie grabbed his hair, not to control but to give himself something to hold on to. Liam sucked the head gently, swirling his tongue around his slit, licking away the beads of precome before the shower spray could.

Hollowing his cheeks, Liam sucked him back down until he bumped the back of his throat, making it constrict. His eyes started to water, but the sounds ripped from Jamie's mouth made him swallow again. He stayed there until his vision blurred, and he pulled off with a gasp, coughing and choking on the water he'd accidentally swallowed.

Jamie gave a shuddering laugh that turned into a groan as Liam closed his fist around him and encouraged him to thrust into it.

There was nothing sexier than seeing Jamie's cock appear and disappear into his palm, to feel the movement of his slick skin against his hand. It was his turn to groan then, and he had to grasp the base of his dick to stop from coming too quickly.

When Jamie's flushed-red tip reappeared in his fist, Liam leaned over and sucked on it slowly, moving his fist down to Jamie's balls. And then Jamie was thrusting into his mouth, catching the back of his throat before pulling back and doing it again.

The sweet, salty taste unique to Jamie coated his tongue and showed him he was close. When Jamie started to pull out again, Liam let his teeth graze gently against his tender length. Jamie gave a strangled scream and pushed back into his mouth so fast that Liam choked as he swallowed around him.

"Sorry," Jamie gasped, but Liam just held on to his bare arse and motioned for him to continue. The roar of the water combined with Jamie's gasps pushed him over the edge, and without even touching his own cock, he spurted between them, crying out around Jamie's erection.

That set Jamie off, and Liam felt his cock pulse in his mouth, and then the strong taste of salt his precome had only teased at. If he could come again, he would have in that moment.

He pulled off Jamie with a gasp, sucking air into his mouth but swallowing water. He coughed, and Jamie helped him to his feet. Both breathless, they kissed, and Jamie curled his tongue into Liam's mouth and tasted himself there.

"Bed?" Liam asked around the kiss.

They cleaned off and stepped out of the shower. Then they dried quickly and fell into bed, hair damp.

Jamie lowered himself over Liam, groin to groin, cocks trapped between their bodies, hot and leaking against each other. "Jamie...." Liam whimpered his name, not knowing what he wanted to say, not knowing what he wanted, but wanting to relay how much he felt.

He hooked his legs around Jamie's hips, not giving him a chance to change his mind, and he welcomed the sharp pain when Jamie's mouth clashed against his, lips pressed against teeth, and Jamie's insistent tongue demanded entrance.

Liam opened his mouth wide, but it still wasn't enough. Jamie's kiss deepened as though he were trying to crawl inside Liam and never leave. Liam wouldn't have minded if he did.

Water trickled down Liam's forehead into his eye, making him blink until he finally closed his eyes and just felt. His bottom lip had split in the onslaught, and Jamie sucked it into his mouth and soothed it with his tongue.

Their groins were still melded together, and Liam's legs started to tremble with the effort to keep them hooked, not wanting to give Jamie a chance to leave. Jamie gave his lip one last suck and then trailed small biting kisses along his jaw and down his neck, sucking as much of the skin into his mouth as he could.

The moist suction of Jamie's mouth and the feel of him working his tongue over Liam's skin as he sucked drove Liam crazy. He had to hold his breath and tense his whole body to stop himself coming from nothing more than a love bite. He usually hated the things, hated how cheap they looked, but Jamie claiming him in that way made his heart swell and his dick leak precome.

Jamie mumbled against Liam's neck, licked strips, and swirled his tongue around the mark he'd just made. Jamie might be smaller than him, but he was wiry and strong. He cupped one of Liam's arse cheeks and changed the angle of their hips so their cocks rubbed against each other. He was happy to let Jamie take charge—wanted it. Sex with other people never felt like this—raw, urgent, and dirty. It was too much, yet not enough.

Jamie crawled backwards down Liam's body, dislodging his legs from his waist. Liam pushed himself up and bit Jamie's collarbone, up and along his jawline, then licked a kiss into his mouth. If he could move his limbs properly, he'd reach for Jamie's dick, but he had no coordination, and all he could do was clutch at Jamie's shoulders, rake his blunt nails down his back, and hope Jamie was feeling as much as Liam was.

This was Jamie's show. Liam knew there was nothing he could do to change that, and he didn't want to. It felt like a claiming, and with each stinging bite, with each word and kiss and touch, his body turned to liquid gold. While his heart rate accelerated, his body was flush from exertion, and his mind had never been so relaxed.

Jamie pushed him back down into the mattress and made his way down Liam's body, leaving no part untouched. Wet kisses glistened all over his skin, and when Jamie finally reached Liam's erection, he cried out and cursed when Jamie didn't touch it, didn't even look at it.

He repositioned Liam's legs and pushed them up to his chest. "Hold them."

Liam grabbed his legs behind the knees, and Jamie shoved his hands under Liam's arse cheeks, pushed them up to his face, and pulled them apart with his thumbs. Liam's face and chest flushed, and his breath hitched as he waited for Jamie to do something—anything. He'd never been so exposed with a lover. He was repelled and drawn the same time. Was Jamie going to?

Jamie nipped one cheek, which made Liam jump, but when he bit the other, he just groaned and pushed back. His hole twitched for something new. Liam was almost desperate with need.

He lifted his head and tried to catch Jamie's eye, but his gaze was firmly on Liam's small ring of muscle. Jamie stretched him wide with his thumbs, and Liam clenched and unclenched, biting back a smile as Jamie groaned and pushed his hips into the bed to find friction.

Liam waited for it, had an idea of what it would feel like. But nothing prepared him for Jamie's hot, wet tongue as he finally licked along the soft crack and brushed it gently over his quivering muscle.

He licked again, and just when Liam tried to lean up so he could grab the back of Jamie's head and push his face where he needed him,

Jamie pressed his lips around him and sucked. Liam flopped back onto the bed and bit back a scream. His skin tingled, and his heart beat so fast he was sure he was going to pass out with it.

Jamie pressed his tongue into him with small, teasing jabs that made his eyes shut and fireworks go off behind his lids. His cock was red and painful. He needed release, yet he never wanted it to end.

Jamie looked around his dick, and Liam blinked at him, trying to keep his eyes open, but finding it difficult. Jamie's eyes were dark and intense, his lips swollen. Liam groaned when he realised why they were swollen.

"Don't come," Jamie said.

How was he supposed to stop it? One movement, one breath, and he would have no control. Liam bit his tongue, the sharp pain something to concentrate on as he tried to do as Jamie asked.

Jamie lowered his head again, and this time he twirled his tongue around his hole. The warmth of his mouth set Liam's nerve endings on fire, and he clenched under the onslaught, feeling empty, needing more.

Each lick or suck sent another round of electricity through Liam's body. His toes and fingers tingled, and he pushed his heels into the mattress to stop himself from coming. There was a point where pleasure could turn to pain, and Liam thought he'd reached it. He wanted to scream at Jamie to stop and then cry if he did and demand he carry on.

Jamie's mouth left him. He sobbed at the empty, cold feeling, and Jamie soothed him with a hand on his leg as he opened a condom. Liam opened his eyes, relieved to see Jamie hadn't left him but wishing they could do it without a barrier. Cooling lube dripped over his crack and trickled down to his hole. Gently Jamie slid his thumb into the gel, spread it around, and then pushed in, just to the first knuckle. Liam was already loose from Jamie's tongue—he was too far gone.

"You look so good from here." Jamie's voice was strained, and Liam leaned up on an elbow to try to see his face, but he was staring so intently at his arse that Liam could only imagine his expression.

It should feel weird, wrong, even, to have someone look at him so intimately and be so turned on, but all it did was make him want more. "Jamie." He couldn't take it—a thumb wasn't enough. A tongue wasn't enough.

Jamie pulled out his thumb, and Liam sobbed, wanting it back. Then Jamie replaced it with a finger and plunged it deeper than the thumb could go, and Liam let out a shuddering breath, fell back down onto the bed, and let his eyelids flutter closed.

"We need to get tested so we can do this bare," Jamie said as he pulled out his fingers and shifted between Liam's legs.

"I thought the same thing." He grabbed Jamie's arm and squeezed as Jamie sank into him. "Yes," he hissed as Jamie's long cock stretched him open and filled him up.

Jamie pulled out gently, almost all the way, and then slammed forward, and Liam saw stars. His eyes rolled back in his head, and he tried to move his hips in time with Jamie's.

Jamie fell over him, keeping most of his weight on his forearms, and Liam moved his head up for a kiss. They kissed messily, open-mouthed, wet—kisses that would put him off with anyone else but were perfection with Jamie.

Each time Jamie's balls slapped against his arse, he let out a whimper that Jamie swallowed up. He'd almost forgotten he had a dick until Jamie gripped it and jacked him so fast he didn't know how to move.

Sensation after sensation hit him from every direction, and he lost the ability to differentiate between them. Heat curled in his gut, and he came with a strangled cry, coating Jamie's fist. Jamie sped up, thrust a few more times, pushed as far into him as he could go, and then fell on top of him. Jamie's dick pulsed inside his arse, and Liam moaned for more.

Jamie was heavy on top of him. Liam's legs were splayed open, and Jamie was slowly softening inside him. It took a few tries for Jamie to reach between them and hold on to the condom as he pulled out.

He didn't even bother taking it off. They were both too drained for anything else. They'd regret it in the morning, but right then, he wanted Jamie splayed on top of him with his come cooling between his legs.

"We need another shower."

"Tomorrow."

# Chapter Twenty-Three

HE MUST have it bad if he was pining because Liam was going away for a measly three days. He was pathetic. Sitting at his mom and dad's kitchen table didn't help either. It made him feel ten years old again. He dunked a digestive biscuit into his tea and took a bite, more to keep distracted than because he wanted one.

"Why didn't you bring Liam with you? Also, what size shoe does he take? I don't want to knit him the wrong size socks."

Jamie's head started to pound. "He's away for the weekend. I promise I'll bring him round soon. And I don't know what shoe size he is." Going by his dick, large, but he wasn't going to say that to her.

"I saw Paul at the supermarket last week."

*Oh God.* "What did you do?"

"I asked him what the hell he and Tommy were playing at, of course. Don't get me wrong, I liked the boy, but I'm not going to bite my tongue."

He cringed, imagining some horrible scene that wouldn't be out of place on *Hollyoaks*. She could be so embarrassing. "You should have ignored him. He's not worth your time."

She glared at him and pointed. "You're my son. He hurt you. I'm not ignoring that."

"So what did he say?" As much as he didn't want his mother fighting his battles, he was interested in what Paul said.

"You know Paul. Always so smooth. Thinks he can charm the birds from the trees. I didn't fall for it, though. I just told him you were better off without them both. He didn't seem too happy about that. He said Liam was your rebound and would never last."

Jamie snorted. Liam may have started off as a rebound, but he wasn't one anymore. It was hard to believe he'd ever thought he was in love with Paul. What he felt for Liam was so much deeper, even if he wasn't ready to say the actual words yet.

He dunked another biscuit into his tea and swore when it broke and plopped into his cup.

"So how serious are you and Liam?" she asked.

"We're serious. I mean… we haven't really talked much about it, but I know." They'd gone to get tested so they could stop using condoms, and they spent most nights together, even with their crazy working hours. He felt more at home with Liam than he ever had with Paul. Liam's presence even made losing Tommy's friendship a little easier to bear. If that wasn't serious, he didn't know what was.

"Marriage serious?" she pressed.

"Mom! We haven't even been together six months yet. Give us a chance. Jesus."

"Okay, okay. No need to get defensive. I only asked. It's not like your sister is ever going to get married. You're my best bet at a big wedding, possibly even grandchildren."

His poor sister. "It's got to be bad if you've got to rely on your gay son for weddings and babies. What did Ellen say to you?"

"You know what she's like. All work, work, work. Back to Liam. Do you love him?"

He flinched at her words and stared down at his tea. "I…. It's new. We're both seeing where it goes." He wanted to say, "Yes, I love him," but they'd never said the words to each other, and he wanted the first time he said them to be to Liam, not to his mom.

Under the table he sent a sneaky *SOS* text to Dane, who rang him almost straightaway and came up with a bullshit story to give Jamie an excuse to leave. Without the cover, she'd keep him there all evening, plying him with biscuits and tea until he couldn't move.

"I'm on my way. No, my mom won't mind. Be there in five." He put the phone down and took his cup to the sink. "I have to go. Dane's had a vet emergency. I'll call you soon, all right? Liam and I will come for dinner." He kissed her on the cheek and fled out the front door, away from her prying.

HE GAVE a quick tap on Dane's front door and let himself in. "Thank you for the save," he called out. Dane was lounging in a large comfortable chair in the corner of his living room, scrolling through his phone.

He grunted in reply and then said, "No wonder your Liam's always so busy. He's busier than me, and I'm a vet on call 24/7."

Liam's voice started to play through the phone, too much like déjà vu for Jamie to be comfortable with. He didn't mind Liam's vlog anymore, but he didn't want any part of it.

He still found himself sitting on the arm of the chair next to Dane, getting sucked up in Liam's antics. He looked good on camera. Jamie could understand why he was popular.

"Are you getting turned on?" Dane asked, wrinkling his nose as they watched Liam bend over to change a tire. "That's gross. If you want to get off to his videos, do it when I'm not here." Dane gave Jamie a shove, and he went sprawling off the side of the chair and landed in an undignified heap.

"Hey! I wasn't getting turned on, thank you very much. I don't need his videos for that. I have the real thing." He didn't even have to pretend to be smug about that.

"God, I hate new relationship fever," Dane scoffed. "He's really popular, did you know that? Even after he stopped those stupid dating videos. Ninety thousand followers. You're dating a celebrity. Well, a minor celeb. B-list at best."

"Gee, thanks. We do like B-films, so I suppose it's fitting. He's at some vloggers' bash in London. Hey, are you busy this weekend? We could have a jamming session at my house."

Dane shrugged his shoulder. "I could be persuaded. Let me check if Markus is free."

"Great." Jamie was relieved not to be spending the weekend alone.

"Aww, that's just too cute for words," Dane said, looking back at one of Liam's videos. "Jesus Christ, is he really washing a car like that, or have I stumbled onto his porn channel?" Dane's eyes were glued to the tiny screen on his phone, and from the laughter and screaming coming from it, it really could be something X-rated.

"Give me that." Jamie snatched the phone out of his hands and saw the glorious image of Liam—his boyfriend—in surfer shorts, flip-flops, that damned *L of a Ride* T-shirt, completely sopping wet. It was so wet it left nothing to the imagination. Shit, he looked hot.

Jamie whimpered a little as Liam leaned forward in the video, showing off his tight arse as he washed his car. It was indecent. Jamie found himself start to get hard and shuffled uncomfortably.

"It *is* porn, isn't it?" Dane bounced, a grin on his face.

Jamie rolled his eyes. "Of course not. It wouldn't be on YouTube if it was." He forced himself to stop watching and scrolled to the description. "It's some kind of challenge for charity. You know, like that Ice Bucket Challenge a while back? Wash your car…. Looks like he had a Just Giving page, and not only did he meet his target of five hundred pounds, he tripled it. In fact, I think it's still up." Jamie clicked on the link, and sure enough, his page was still there and people were still donating, though not as often as before.

"It's to raise money for something called Waardenburg Syndrome." Jamie donated £20 and put little heart emojis in the comment box. "I donated. You should too."

Dane cackled and took his phone back. "He's so gonna know you were stalking his page."

Jamie blushed at the thought but didn't think Liam would mind or think it was strange. He had a business that sounded more like a porn video, for Christ's sake. "Shut up. He'll be happy because it means I've been using social media, and he's trying to persuade me it isn't as evil as I think it is." It was sort of working.

"Terrible comeback, my dear, terrible. Anyway, now I've saved you from your dear, well-meaning mother, you should leave. I've got enough material here to fund my fantasies for at least three weeks." Dane sounded entirely too pleased with himself.

"Please don't masturbate while watching innocent videos of my boyfriend."

"See you later, darling," Dane said, curling into his chair.

"You, Daniel Vincent, are a terrible human being." Jamie pointed his finger at him, let himself out, and bumped into Ben as he did.

"Ben? Hi?" Jamie was confused to see his work colleague at Dane's. He didn't even think they were that close.

Ben blushed and looked into the house. "Er, hi, Jamie. I'm just…. Dane?"

Dane padded barefoot to the front door and smiled when he saw Ben. "Ben, darling. Come on in. Jamie was just leaving." He kissed Ben on the cheek and pulled him over the threshold. Ben looked back over his shoulder at Jamie, a small frown on his face.

Well, that was interesting. Jamie looked back at Dane's house one more time and then went home to give it a bit of a clean before they guys came around and trashed it.

# Chapter Twenty-Four

IT WAS strange to be with all these people who knew him mostly as the playboy who used every opportunity to try to get someone into bed, and then vlogged about it. Things were different this time.

He missed Jamie and the rats. He was having fun catching up, but he knew he'd be having more fun at home. Jamie promised he could have one of Agatha's kittens, so he was ecstatic about that. And there was no one here he could talk to about the rats. It was odd to feel so alone with a group of people he considered his friends. He wanted to be on the sofa watching the rest of *Lexx and the Dark Zone* stories. He wanted to start watching the original *Beauty and the Beast* TV series.

Nearly everyone was talking into their cameras for their own vlogs, but he just couldn't find the energy for it. Some were doing it in tandem, and Liam felt a bit out of the loop.

"It's not completely different," Tabitha said to him. She was a lifestyle vlogger who concentrated mostly on vintage clothing and upcycling. "You're going back to where you started. Your vlog is part lifestyle, part informative. People like that…. Some people. You'll find your groove." He wished he was as sure as she was. She wandered off to speak to someone else, and Liam thankfully had a second of quiet.

There were a few more people there he didn't recognise, but he pasted on his smile and went to socialise. Someone he didn't know came up to him.

"Hi," he said, surprised when she signed it back to him.

*My name is Abigail*, she said. Then she showed him her nickname.

He signed slowly at first, unsure how fluent she was, but she understood everything, so he relaxed and stared as his hands quickened.

She had her own vlog about her life as a deaf music lover. She signed or added sign to each of her videos, and he loved speaking with her and getting her input. She might have been young, but she was doing something similar to what he wanted to do.

She'd also heard of his favourite singer, Phase, and they geeked out about him like typical fangirls. She loved loud experimental music she could feel the vibrations for, and she also loved how Phase dressed like he didn't give a shit about what anyone thought. Liam liked that about him too.

Abi had even been sponsored by various online BSL courses, which was a direction he hadn't even thought of and one that excited him.

"Speak English, I can't understand!" A makeup vlogger he remembered from last year jumped on his back with a laugh, making Abi flinch. Liam stumbled forward, grabbed the legs at his sides to stop them both falling. He let him slide down his back and stepped away from him quickly.

*Sorry*, he signed to Abi and then turned around. "That was fucking rude. I was in the middle of a conversation."

The guy pouted and flicked his long hair over his shoulder. "I haven't seen you in ages, and I couldn't understand a word you were saying. You weren't even signing and talking."

"Because I didn't need to. We understood each other perfectly. Maybe you should say sorry for being so rude."

He glared at them and muttered, "Sorry."

Liam shook his head. "Not like that. Like this." He made a loose fist with his right hand and moved it in a circle over his chest. "It's easy."

The man glared at Abigail, who was looking at them through her hair, clearly uncomfortable. But he copied what Liam had done. Abigail nodded and signed *thank you*, and he flounced off.

*Sorry about that.*

*Don't worry about it. Some people just love being centre of attention.*

They spoke for a few more minutes, exchanged social media details, and then Abi's friends dragged her away to find food.

Michael Carson, aka MC Glamour Time on YouTube, was one of his closest YouTube friends and was always available for a hookup. He looked as good as he always did. A hairdresser in real life, he always had a new hairdo or colour, and he always dressed brilliantly, with a unique style that reminded Liam of a Punk Hippy. He was a bit too much of a diva for Liam, but they'd always got on well.

Liam was single the last time they met, and he wasn't sure of his reception now. It was the first time he'd been to a vlogger party while attached, and it was odd—good but odd. He wished Jamie were there. It would make everything so much easier. He found himself wanting to tell everyone about Jamie.

"Liam, sweetie." Michael waved at him from across the room and danced his way through everyone until he was right in front of him. He pressed a kiss slick with gloss to Liam's lips, and Liam just wiped it off with the back of his hand with a laugh but otherwise didn't mention it. Michael greeted everyone the same way.

"MC, how are you?"

"I am good, as you very well know, if you'd been watching my videos as religiously as I watch yours." He leaned in closer and gripped the sleeve of his T-shirt. "We're not here to talk about me, you sneaky boy. We're here to talk about tall, dark, and mysterious. Gossip, please. It must be serious for you to change your whole Tube around."

Liam's whole body relaxed, and he couldn't stop the huge smile that took over his face. It was nice to know Michael wouldn't be expecting anything more than gossip from him, and Jamie was one of his favourite subjects. "It's good to know you're still watching my videos. Jamie is amazing."

"Young love. It's delightfully sickening, but I am so pleased for you." He gave Liam a tight hug that almost cracked his ribs. Then he stared at Liam's face intently and turned it one way and then the other, as though seeing something he didn't quite like. "Well, I can tell you're not watching my videos. Your eyebrows are out of control. You simply must let me tidy them before you go home."

# Chapter Twenty-Five

PLAYING HIS favourite songs on the uke put Jamie in a good mood. He was by no means an expert—none of them were—but they all had fun and occasionally got to pretend to be rock stars.

They sat in the living room, and Jamie tuned his uke while Markus and Dane argued over what song to play next. He rolled his eyes at them and quickly started to pluck out a tune to get them to pay attention.

It was a song from Liam's favourite singer and not one they'd played before. It took a second for them to get the rhythm of it, and then they joined in, Dane attempting to sing the lyrics, making them up when he couldn't remember them.

What started out as a jamming session turned into a small party when Jamie's sister turned up and Dane casually threw in that Ben might also be stopping by. Jamie didn't know what was going on between those two, and it was none of his business, so he tried not to pry, even though he desperately wanted to know.

They'd been drinking, and he was lightly buzzed. His fingers were tingling from practicing, and the only thing that made it not perfect was that Liam wasn't there. He should have demanded to go along with him—not because he didn't trust Liam, but because he missed him. He was like a lovestruck teenager.

"Why are you frowning?" his sister slurred, pointing at him with an accusing finger. He stopped playing.

"Ooh, I know," Dane said, seamlessly going from singing to talking. He raised his hand as though he were a kid at school, uke lying across his lap. "He misses *Liam*." He said his name in a sing-song voice that Markus cackle.

Jamie couldn't even argue with him because it was true. "I hate you all."

"You are so drunk right now. Don't worry, I won't hold it against you at work." Ben winked. Any awkwardness dissolved due to the joys of alcohol. Jamie noticed how obvious he and Dane were being about not talking much to each other and found it confusing.

"You boys need to give me all the gossip about Liam. I haven't even met him yet, and my brother is being very quiet." Ellen poked him in the ribs and made his uke slip off his lap. He managed to grab it before it hit the floor, but it was a close call. He placed it on the coffee table with the gentleness that only came with having one too many beers.

He didn't spend a lot of time with his sister. They were both busy with work and trying to avoid their mother, which was a full-time job in itself. "Don't poke me, woman. Do you want me to throw up on you? Besides, I don't want to scare Liam away," he said dryly. "He's met Mom. We're both still recovering."

"Well, I, for one, am happy you've taken the heat off me. Carry on what you're doing. You have the wedding and the babies, and she'll leave me in peace. So, Dane, is this Liam good enough for our Jamie?"

"He hasn't cheated on our boy yet, and he seems just as smitten, so I'd say that's a success," Dane said as he topped up her glass.

"Definitely what I like to hear. I never really thought Jamie and Paul were a good fit. It was so... on the surface, wouldn't you say?"

Jamie cleared his throat, and they both looked at him as though they were surprised he was listening to their conversation. "*He* is here, you know."

Dane smirked at him and leaned toward Ellen. "I'd say Jamie's most definitely on the surface with Liam, darling." He pointed to the sofa. "That surface—" Then to the coffee table. "That surface. I don't think there's a lot of surfaces they haven't been on." He wiggled his eyebrows, and Jamie groaned in embarrassment and closed his eyes so he couldn't see them cackle together like naughty schoolchildren.

"Please stop talking about me like I'm not here. I need more alcohol," Jamie muttered. He went into the kitchen in search of something stronger than wine and beer and to get out of earshot. He didn't want to listen to them all talk about him. His cheeks burned, but he couldn't even pretend to protest because it was the truth. He *did* turn into a lovesick fool around Liam, and they *had* fucked on and against many surfaces, not that Dane knew that for sure.

The doorbell rang, and Markus hollered that he'd get it, so Jamie was free to break out the vodka. "If it's the Jehovah's Witnesses again, ask them in for a threesome," he called out. Maybe it was Liam and he'd forgotten his key. He'd get a kick out of his lame joke if it was. The bottle of vodka was half-empty, but there would be enough to create a nice little buzz for them all.

He searched for shot glasses and carried them into the living room. It took him much too long to realise that the atmosphere in the living room had changed, and it wasn't Liam who had been at the door.

"What the fuck are *you* doing here?" Jamie glared at Markus for letting him in. He at least had the sense to look guilty and uncomfortable.

Markus shrugged in helplessness. "Sorry, mate. I didn't know what to do."

"Maybe tell him to fuck off?"

Paul stood in front of the fireplace, looking completely at home. He touched the ornaments and trinkets lined up on the shelf above, then put them down in the wrong place, which made Jamie want to scream at him. He acted as though he still lived there and had the right to touch what he wanted. Jamie ground his teeth together and slammed the bottle and glasses onto the table.

Paul didn't even flinch.

Paul rolled his eyes and gave a short high-pitched laugh that made Jamie wince. "Come on. Surely it's time to put the past in the past and let bygones be bygones?"

As usual Paul looked perfectly pressed in a neat lemon shirt, black jeans, braces, and a bow tie. His hair was styled into a small quiff with a bit of wax to give it some texture. There was a slight strain around his eyes that told Jamie he wasn't as comfortable as he wanted them to believe, and that reason, more than anything else, turned his anger down a notch. He was glad Paul was uncomfortable. What ex in their right mind would turn up on the doorstep of the boyfriend they'd dumped and act as if nothing were wrong?

"What are you doing here?" Jamie repeated. "Where's Tommy?" Jamie glanced toward the door, expecting to see Tommy walk up the driveway after finding somewhere to park.

"He's at his parents'. I was bored rattling around on my own. Remember when we all used to go out partying? We had fun, didn't we? We could all have fun again." There was a hint of desperation in his voice, but Jamie wasn't going to let that fool him. Paul was used to being the centre of attention.

It was probably why he'd turned up. He was a master manipulator. Jamie could see that now that he wasn't in the thick of it.

"We're not friends, Paul. Boyfriends don't cheat with their boyfriend's best friend. They don't cheat at all. We might know the same people, you might be fucking Tommy now, but I'm not your friend, and I'm not his either. So. Why. Are. You. Here?"

Paul's shoulders drooped, and he frowned and looked to the floor. It all seemed a little too perfect to Jamie, but there was still a part of him that was unsure if it was an act or not. "Tom's parents don't like me." Jamie bit the inside of his cheek to stop himself from smirking in satisfaction. Tommy's parents loved *him*. "I just wanted things to be how they used to be, back when we were all friends and everything was simpler."

"Go to the village. I'm sure you'll get plenty of attention there." Jamie didn't like having this conversation with an audience, but he didn't want to speak with Paul alone either. They'd said everything they needed to say when Paul collected all his belongings.

"It's not the same."

"You should have thought about that before you hurt my brother," Ellen chimed in, and Paul's eyes widened.

"Ellen, it's... good to see you."

She stood on unsteady feet and stepped in front of him. "It's really not," she said. Jamie had no clue what she was up to, and he jumped when she pulled her hand back and slapped Paul across the face. Paul teetered on his feet and grabbed his cheek as his mouth fell open in shock. "That's for what you did to my brother."

It was all Jamie could do not to cheer out loud.

Paul straightened and pressed his lips together. He shoved his hands in his pockets and looked at them all in turn. "I'll go. For what it's worth, I'm sorry I hurt you, but you weren't perfect either." He took a step toward the door, then hesitated and looked backwards. "It looks different in here." He motioned around the room.

Jamie frowned in confusion. "I don't know what you mean." He couldn't think of anything that had changed since Paul lived there.

"You let Liam hang his jumper over the banister. There's one of his shoes over there. You always bitched if I did that. You never let me put my mark on this place."

Jamie blinked as he realised Liam had indeed left a jumper abandoned on the banister when the coat hook was only on the opposite wall. Had he really moaned at Paul for doing the same thing? He couldn't recall.

"It's just stuff," he said, though he knew it wasn't. Liam's jumper gave him a warm feeling inside. He itched to slip it on so he could be surrounded by Liam's scent, but that would give more weight to Paul's words.

Paul let out an angry laugh. "Of course it is. Fuck you all. I don't need any of you. No need to see me out; I know where the door is." He stormed out of the living room and down the hallway. They all heard the front door slam as he left.

"Well, he was a box of delights," Ellen said as she sat back down. "Is that vodka? I think this deserves a shot or two for everyone, don't you think?"

Everyone agreed, and Jamie poured out the drinks. He tried to ignore Paul's interruption but was unable to stop thinking about what he'd said. Liam didn't even live there officially, but wherever he looked, Jamie was reminded of him.

"I like it," Jamie said, looking around with a new eye and noticing everything that had turned it into a home and not just a house.

"What are you talking about?" Markus asked.

"Stuff. Liam's stuff here, mingling with mine. I like it." He knocked back a shot and poured another. "Anyone hungry? I've got Doritos and possibly Pringles." If Liam hadn't eaten them before leaving. A curry or chips would be better, but he couldn't be bothered to make a run into town. Crisps would have to do.

"I could eat," Dane said. "Need a hand?"

"To put Doritos in a bowl and hunt for Pringles?" He laughed. "No, I'm good."

"Bring in another bottle of wine, would you?" Ellen said.

He saluted her, walked into the kitchen, and opened the fridge to find the bottle of Lambrini in there for when Liam and Selena were around. For some reason they had never grown out of drinking it like most sane people did.

He balanced bowls, dip, and a bottle of wine in his hands and walked through the doorway back to the living room. He felt a draught, glanced toward the front door, and cursed. Paul had left it open. Another mark against him. He put the snacks down on the cluttered coffee table and quickly went back to shut it.

JAMIE WOKE the next morning to the smell of bacon and the taste of death in his mouth. His head thumped with every breath, and his stomach churned. Maybe he would die, and then the pain would stop. That sounded like a good plan.

When death didn't take him, he gingerly got out of bed and grabbed Liam's dressing gown—the white one he'd had *L of a Ride* embroidered on the breast pocket of as a joke—and followed the salty scent of bacon, needing to soak up the alcohol.

Ellen looked as bad as he did. Her eyeliner was smudged around her eyes, she still had bed hair, and the look on her face said that only bacon could cure how awful she felt. He understood.

"Bacon-and-egg buttie?" she asked. He grunted a response and put the kettle on for tea. He wished he'd had enough about him to brush his teeth before coming downstairs, but he didn't have the energy to go all the way back up there to do it.

"I'll bring Liam around to meet you when he gets back. Maybe next week?" How good was he? Having a proper conversation. He could do this. He wasn't hungover at all. Not one bit.

She shook her head and then retched at the sudden movement. "Jesus Christ, I feel like shit. I'm away for work next week. The week after for definite, though."

Ellen cooking him breakfast reminded him of being a teenager again and how they used to go out on the lash, get back in so late that not even their mother could nag them enough to get out of bed, and then they'd have a fry-up for lunch. Those were good times, back when he could take his alcohol.

"Smashing," he said as she put a plate in front of him and sat opposite to eat her own. "What are you up to for the rest of the day?"

"I need to get sorted for next week, but I really want to go home and die." She pulled a face and took a big bite of her sandwich. "I haven't drunk that much in ages."

"You're more than welcome to help me clean out the rats." He wanted them to all look perfect for when Liam got back, but he wasn't looking forward to that chore. It was a mammoth task with the number of rats he had.

Ellen snorted. "No, thanks. I cleaned them out enough when we were kids and I lost those stupid bets to you. Anyway, I have to go as soon as I've finished this." She ate her sandwich in a few bites as Jamie took delicate nibbles, trying to calm his queasy stomach. "I'll see you soon? Text me."

Jamie nodded and stood up long enough to kiss her on the cheek. "Definitely. Thanks for the bacon."

"No problem. It was your bacon. I just grilled it. Don't bother getting up, I can see myself out."

"Bye, bye. Love you," he called as he settled back into the chair and ate the rest of his breakfast.

One he'd eaten, he felt almost human. Almost. Human enough to send Liam a photo of the state of the living room, his poor abandoned uke lying amidst it all. It was carnage. Liam sent a gif back of a troll riding a train. Jamie hoped that meant he was on his way back already.

It made him smile as he tried to tidy, but he didn't get very far because he kept stopping for a breather and getting sidetracked by whatever crap was on the TV.

Bottles were finally in the recycling bin, and he'd swept as many of the bits up as possible. Deeming that good enough, he went back upstairs. He desperately wanted a long, hot shower, but there was no point in showering before he cleaned the rats out.

He opened the rat room, said hello to all the little faces that peered up at him. Agatha was out of her nest, the babies all surrounding her now they had their eyes open and were big enough to run around. They were growing strong, their coats coming in glossy and healthy. It was difficult to decide which ones he would keep, but he had a while to decide which were the best.

Liam's rats were in the spare cage on top of the dresser, full of substrate and food. He went over to them. Mabel and Maud were lounging in the *Ghostbuster* hammock at the top, both grinding their teeth when they heard his voice.

"Missing your dad, huh? Me too," he said as he opened their cage.

Upon hearing his voice, Gert poked her head out of the plastic house on the bottom of the cage and ambled out. She sniffed at the bars and looked forlornly at him. Unable to resist her cute face, he picked her up for a quick cuddle, scratched her back, and tickled between her ears.

"Like that, do you? Yeah, your dad does too." Jamie smirked. But as he went to put Gert back, he saw a blue blur from the corner of his eye, and he jumped back, heart in his mouth.

Gert wriggled in his hands, and it was only years of experience that kept him from dropping her. He lurched back toward the cage, eyes blinking in case he was seeing things. The alcohol had obviously addled his brain.

Then he went ice cold all over, hairs on his arms standing on end. He shivered, teeth chattering, and his stomach roiled.

"What the fuck?" he said. There were a couple of things Jamie always prided himself on—meticulous breeding and being a reliable boarder. This showed neither of those traits.

The shock of what he saw had him rooted to the spot, and it was only when one of the rats climbed out of the hammock—a rat that most definitely should not be in that cage—that he sprang to action. He quickly put Gert in the top of the cage with her sisters and then scooped Negan out. All the while, his heart thumped painfully in his chest.

Negan was a large Russian Blue buck with a bossy personality to match his namesake, though he wasn't half so cruel—luckily. He lay in Jamie's two hands, his body relaxed, eyes boggling. "Yeah, no wonder you're boggling, you devil."

Negan went back with his cage mates, no worse for wear. Jamie could not get his head around it. The bacon churned in his stomach, and acid burned the back of his throat. He bit his lips, willing his body not to betray him.

"Shit. Shit, fuck." How long had Negan been in their cage, and more importantly, how did he get there? There was no way he would have mistaken the cages—he couldn't have been that drunk, could he? He wracked his brain, trying to remember what happened the night before, but he couldn't, for the life of him, remember going into the rat room after everyone left.

He took a deep breath. He needed to concentrate on the here and now. Whatever he'd done last night wasn't as important as checking the girls for any injuries. They looked no worse for wear, sitting in their hammocks, but rats were prey animals and generally hid any hurt they might have. Forming a plan, he nodded—check the rats now, panic later. His hands shook as he checked each one of them and only found one small scratch on Maud.

He checked the rest of the cages, made sure each rat was in the right place, and breathed a sigh of relief when they were. Dread settled over him like a weighted blanket, making it hard to breath. What was he meant to do now?

Fleetingly he thought about pretending it hadn't happened, but just the thought crippled him with guilt. He couldn't do that to Liam. He closed his eyes and whimpered. What would everyone in the rat community say? How was Jan going to look at him after this? If this mistake resulted in an "oops" litter—or three—he'd never live it down.

It was very possible that all three rats could now end up pregnant, and that would make him look like an amateur and could seriously undermine his business. He tasted the bacon at the back of his throat and swallowed, trying to calm his stomach again.

How was he going to tell Liam? *Hey, honey, I'm glad you're back. We're going to be rat fathers because I accidently put my prize Russian Blue buck in with your pride and joy rescues?*

The only positive he could think of was at least it was Liam's rats and not a boarder's. He felt guilty for thinking it, but it was true. If he could persuade Liam to take them to see Dane at the practice, then he could give them something to prevent pregnancy. The last thing either of them needed was thirty-plus rat kittens. Liam would see reason. Now if only Jamie could remember how it happened.

He went in search of his phone and rang Dane, cursing when he didn't answer right away. "Come on, Dane, answer, damn you...." What the hell was he doing? He never took so long answering.

"What are you ringing me so early for?" Thank God. It didn't matter that Dane was grumpy; that was typical Dane. Jamie tried to laugh, but it turned into a sob. "What is it, what's wrong?" The grumpiness disappeared, and Dane sounded fully alert.

"I fucked up, Dane." His hangover chose that moment to come back with a vengeance, and he dropped his mobile and leaned forward as vomit sprayed from between his lips and soaked into the carpet in front of him.

Dane was there fifteen minutes later, wearing jogging bottoms and a creased T-shirt. Jamie had never seen him so rumpled, even when they lived together at uni. Dane picked him up off the floor in much the same manner he did a foal and then manhandled him into the shower.

"Shower. I'll stand just outside in case you need help. Then you can tell me what's happened."

Jamie clutched the doorframe, sweat beading on his forehead. He must look a mess. He certainly felt it, and he knew it wasn't all because of the hangover. "I'll be fine. Can you check on Liam's rats? I found Negan in their cage this morning."

Dane literally flinched, and his mouth dropped open. "What the hell?"

"I don't know. I have no clue. Can you check them for me?" Dane nodded and left him in the bathroom. Jamie took a deep breath, leaned over the sink, turned on the cold tap, and drank straight from it. It made his mouth feel marginally less like death.

When he'd finally showered and dressed, he went to find Dane. His hair was still wet, and droplets trailed down his neck and wet his T-shirt. He shivered at the cold but didn't bother trying to towel it dry. Dane was on his hands and knees, cleaning up Jamie's vomit.

"You didn't have to do that."

Dane glanced up but didn't stop scrubbing. "Don't worry. Call us even for that time I puked in your car." He wrung out the sponge, scrubbed one last time, and peeled the rubber gloves off. "I'll just get rid of this and be right back."

Jamie heard the toilet flush and the tap turn on before Dane came back.

"Physically the girls are fine, but you might want to bring them to the surgery for Galastop."

A shot of relief surged through him. That was right. If they did that, then everything would be fine. "I'll have to explain to Liam." Dane nodded. "How the hell do I make this be all right?" Whatever he said to Liam, it would be bad. If only he could turn back the clock.

"Come on. Let's go down to the living room and you can tell me all about it."

The living room was still mostly a mess from their impromptu party the night before. Jamie wished it hadn't happened, that they hadn't even had band practice. He brushed some crumbs off the sofa and practically collapsed into it. "How come you don't have a hangover?"

Dane raised an eyebrow. "You know I don't get hangovers, darling. Plus I didn't drink as much as you."

"I can't even remember half of last night. What did I do?"

"Nothing that I saw. Are you going to tell me what happened? This isn't like you at all. You're so sensible."

Sensible. Boring. The reason Paul left him. The reason he tried to keep the peace for the sake of their friends. Well, no one could call him boring now. "I don't remember getting Negan out and putting him in with the girls. I'd remember that, wouldn't I?" There was a bad taste in his mouth, and it had nothing to do with throwing up earlier. Self-loathing made his chest ache until he could barely breathe.

"I'm sure Liam will understand when you explain."

"How can I explain when I don't remember? I'm going to look such a fool. They'll never ask me to judge again."

Dane gave him a hug. "Liam will be back soon. Speak to him first, then worry about everyone else. You're only human, darling. We all make mistakes."

If only he could get away saying nothing. Putting his head in the sand sounded like a pretty good idea right then.

# Chapter Twenty-Six

THE TRAIN ride home was long, boring, and cramped. Liam's arse became numb and it was impossible to sleep. He'd enjoyed the weekend away, but he was ready to get home to Jamie. Next year, he decided, he would ask Jamie to go with him. He couldn't stop the smile when he thought about next year. Who would have thought he would settle down? Not him. He shuddered when he thought about what he used to get up to before he met Jamie. He'd been so sure he was having fun and enjoying life, but he was just making a mockery of it.

The train stopped at every station. It took over two hours for him to get back, and the relief washed over him. When he finally reached his stop, he grabbed his bag and made his way to the taxi rank. It wasn't that far to Jamie's, but he couldn't face the half-hour walk.

His car was parked on the curb outside Jamie's house, the *L* plates tucked in the boot, waiting for his student tomorrow morning. He'd moved a lot of students around to have the full weekend off, so next week was going to be busy catching up.

Jamie's house was quiet when he let himself in. The living room looked like an attempt had been made to tidy it, but it was a half-hearted try at best. Jamie must be feeling worse for wear—possibly still nursing a hangover in bed.

"Jamie?" Liam called softly. He poked his head into the kitchen and, seeing it empty, made his way back upstairs. The door to the rat room was open, and knowing Jamie wouldn't leave it unattended with Stark in the house, he figured Jamie would be with the rats.

He wasn't wrong, although he was surprised to see him still in Liam's dressing gown, sitting cross-legged on the floor with his head in his hands. His head shot up when Liam padded into the room, and Liam's smile started to slip. Something was wrong.

"Are you okay?"

Jamie looked green around the gills and bit his lip nervously. He got to his feet, knees cracking, and his gaze flitted to Liam's rats behind him. "I can explain. The girls are fine."

He twisted around in alarm, hands against the bars as he looked from one rat to the other. "What do you mean?"

Jamie stood up and cupped his elbow. "I said they're okay. There was just a—mishap."

Liam frowned. He didn't like the sound of that, and Jamie's body language didn't match his words. It tied his stomach in knots. "Whenever someone starts a conversation like that, it doesn't usually mean 'fine.' What's wrong?"

Jamie's face screwed up, lips pursed tightly. Then he forced out a deep breath. "I don't know how it happened, but somehow, Negan ended up in their cage—"

"What?" Negan? He was at least three times bigger than each girl. Liam quickly opened the cage. Jamie could tell him they were fine until he was blue in the face, but until he'd seen each toe, inspected each whisker, and kissed each furry belly, he couldn't be sure. "What the hell happened?"

"I have no bloody idea. I don't know how I could have put him in the wrong cage. In all my time keeping rats, that has never happened before." Jamie stared over to Negan's cage and back as though trying to bring back the memory of what had happened but drawing a blank.

Liam pressed his lips together, fingernails biting into the palms of his hands. As explanations went, it was a shitty one.

"It'll be fine. All we have to do is take them to see Dane. He'll give them something to prevent pregnancy."

Liam's head jerked back as he tried to read Jamie's eyes. "Wait, what?" He must be slow, because when he'd heard Negan was in the cage with the girls, he thought about fighting rather than pregnancies.

Jamie swallowed and turned away, fiddling with the belt on the dressing gown. "It won't hurt them. It'll just make sure there are no unplanned litters. Shit, I don't know how this happened. I don't do things like this. I'm careful." Jamie bit his lips until they bled.

Liam knew how careful he was, how he carefully planned each litter. He was shocked and a little hurt, if he was being honest with himself. He'd trusted Jamie. He couldn't understand why babies would be such a terrible thing. Jamie was a rat breeder; there were always rat kittens in his house.

"Babies?" He loved Agatha's kittens, and he'd helped look after them. He'd love to look after any kittens his girls might have.

Jamie rubbed his hand down his face. "Don't sound like that—all hopeful and excited. This is bad, Bowie. I fucked up." He swallowed, and his eyes filled with tears.

"Okay. You fucked up. But you have litters all the time. You take in rescue litters. How is this any different?"

"It's very different. It's not planned. No breeder breeds using rescue rats. There are too many unknowns. I've worked so hard to be a serious breeder. I'll be a laughingstock." Jamie's voice sounded panicked.

"Because you're is what's important here." Jamie winced, but Liam was too mad to feel sorry for him.

"There are so many things that could go wrong. They're rescues. They could have health problems we don't even know about. Maud and Gert are still so young." Jamie ran a hand through his hair, fingers tangling in his damp locks.

"Maud and Gert's mom was fine, and Mabel probably came from a breeding farm, and she survived."

Jamie cleared his throat. "It would be wrong of us to bring more rats into the world. We should take them to see Dane."

Liam gave a bitter laugh and shook his head. "Oh, you've got it all planned out, haven't you? What if I don't want to?"

"You could end up with over thirty rats." It did sound daunting when he put it like that. "It's insane. Surely you see that?" Jamie said.

Liam swallowed the lump in his throat. Why was Jamie having a go at him? He wasn't the one that fucked up, so why was he making Liam feel like he was in the wrong for wanting to wait and see what happened? This wasn't the Jamie he knew and loved. Had he been taken over by aliens or something? Because the Jamie he knew wouldn't act like this.

"I don't see anything insane," Liam said, crossing his arms over his chest.

"They could end up pregnant." Jamie spoke slowly, as though he thought Liam didn't understand. "If that happens, you can't tell anyone it happened here. Not in person or on your vlog. No one would trust me again. My reputation will be ruined." Jamie said. He looked horrified at the prospect, and that made Liam even more angry. He should be worried about the rats, not himself. Jamie was usually the least selfish person he knew, but right now the only person Jamie cared about was Jamie.

"Do you even care about the rats, or are you more worried about yourself?"

Jamie gave an angry burst of laughter. "Don't be silly, of course not. I love all of our rats, but I'm a professional breeder. You wouldn't understand."

"What's that supposed to mean?" Liam glared at Jamie, but he didn't notice as he carried on.

"Come on, Liam. Your own reputation is a joke. It's based around making a tit of yourself on YouTube. There's no way you could know what this means to me or how it could damage me if it gets out. I mean, you don't even take being a driving instructor seriously."

Liam flinched "What are you talking about?" He felt like he'd been punched in the stomach. Was that really what Jamie thought of him? "You obviously don't know me at all if that's what you think." Didn't Jamie see the long hours he put in? The unsocial hours kept so he could work around his students' studies and jobs? How long he would stay up editing videos?

Despite his laid-back persona, he took his work very seriously. He was good at what he did, and he enjoyed it. He wouldn't have lasted as long as he had if he didn't. Being self-employed was tough. That was something Jamie wouldn't understand.

Jamie rolled his eyes. "What small business owner calls their company *L of a Ride* unless they're a prostitute? It's ridiculous. You spend countless hours messing about with your vlog. Everything is one big joke."

That stung. Liam blinked. This was messed up. How had they gone from Jamie messing up to picking apart Liam's life? "Fuck you. I take it all seriously. We've never really talked about money, have we? But I make money vlogging. Not a huge amount, but the more work I put in 'messing about,' as you delightfully put it, the more I'll make. And the name of my business, that you apparently hate? I get bookings just because people see my car and remember the name, so fuck you, Jamie, fuck you. I have a business degree. I'm not some dumb blond."

This wasn't what Liam expected to come home to. He'd missed Jamie so much, he just wanted to get back and fall into his arms. But now all he wanted was to get away from him.

"Don't take it like that. You've got to admit it's—" Jamie's face went white. "Shit. It was Paul." He gave a laugh. "Fucking bastard."

"Paul?" Liam asked, confused. He was having trouble keeping up with the stream of conversation and insults that Jamie threw his way.

"Yes, *Paul*. He took too long in the toilet, but I never thought anything at the time." Jamie sounded relieved, but Liam felt anything but.

"Paul was here?" There was a sour taste in Liam's mouth at the mention of Jamie's ex, and he couldn't stop the jealousy leaking into his words. Wasn't it enough that he had to put up with Paul when they were out with Jamie's friends? "*Paul* was here?"

"*Yes*. I didn't invite him, he just turned up."

"Yet you didn't turn him away? *Come on*. Your ex ended up at your house—the house he used to live in with you. The guy you thought you'd spend the rest of your life with, the guy who slept with your best mate and broke up with you at a pet rat show?" The green-eyed monster grew as he pictured Paul in Jamie's home—the home Liam had started to feel so comfortable in.

"Are you implying I wanted him here? I've been trying to keep the peace since he fucked me over. I didn't ask him in, but I couldn't cause a scene either. At least we know it wasn't my fault now, I didn't switch the rats."

Liam gave a dry, painful laugh. It wasn't even about the rats anymore. Jamie put everyone before Liam—including himself. How could he trust him? Not just because of Paul, but because of Jamie's true feelings about Liam's career path. "Good for you. You can tell that to all your rat friends, I'm sure that will save your pristine reputation. I'll go back to my whoring around."

Liam couldn't believe what he'd walked into. He started to gather the girls' things, shoving treats and food into a bag. His eyes burned with angry tears, but he refused to let them fall. Jamie couldn't even see how much his words hurt.

What was the saying? *Sticks and stones may hurt my bones, but words will never hurt me*? That was a pile of shit. Jamie's words hurt more than Liam knew how to deal with. The only thing he knew for sure was he had to leave the house and get as far away from Jamie as he could.

Was Liam being unreasonable? Was he in the wrong? Jamie basically shit on all his accomplishments. He was damned proud of being a driving instructor. He was proud of his vlog—even the dating disasters, because his channel would never have evolved without it.

"Where are you going? Don't leave. We still need to talk about this." Jamie grabbed his arm, and Liam shrugged it off and opened the pet carrier.

"I'm going home." He felt bruised all over; skin too tight for his bones, and his face ached from trying to stop any kind of emotion other than anger showing.

"Don't be unreasonable. I've said I'm sorry."

Liam's mouth dropped open. "Me unreasonable? You apparently hate everything about me. What do you even see in me, or am I still that rebound boyfriend you keep around so you can pretend to Paul and the rest of your friends that you're over him?"

"Don't be stupid. I'm not pining after Paul, but I can't make it awkward for our mutual friends either." The same old story again.

Liam gave him a pointed look and put the rats into the carrier. "Could have fooled me. What am I supposed to think when he turns up the weekend I'm gone, and this happens?" He shut the lid and picked up the handle. "Did he warm your bed too?" Liam didn't really believe that Jamie had slept with Paul, but he did want to hurt him as much as he was hurting.

"I wouldn't do that. I'm sorry, okay. I'm hungover, I feel like shit, and I can't have this getting out. I've already been humiliated in front of the rat community. I can't have this getting out." Liam walked toward the door. He was so done. "Let's talk about this," Jamie pleaded.

"You've done enough talking. You should worry about your precious reputation instead."

"Please, we haven't finished." Jamie's voice was high-pitched and shaky. "Don't leave. We need to call Dane, at the very least." Liam pushed the hurt down and concentrated on the anger as it uncurled inside him. He glared at Jamie, not liking him very much right then.

"We're done talking. You worry about your rats, and I'll worry about mine."

"Don't be like that. You know I love the girls. I just don't want anyone to question my ethics."

"I'm questioning your ethics right now." Liam shook his head, hair falling into his eyes. "Perhaps you're not as decent a breeder as you thought you were." Jamie flinched, and Liam had a moment of satisfaction before jogging out to his car and driving away. He could break down when he got home.

# Chapter Twenty-Seven

SURELY HE could have one day of self-pitying isolation where he got to stay in bed and no one bothered him? "It's been two weeks, not one day," the voice said, and Jamie hadn't realised he'd even said anything aloud.

"Fuck off." The duvet was ripped from over his head, and he managed to grab the corner and yank it back, but it was soon ripped off again. Grudgingly he opened one eye and blinked up at the figure looming over him. "I'm trying to sleep."

Dane raised an eyebrow and threw the quilt onto the floor. *Bastard.* "Yes. For the past *two weeks*. I know what you're doing, and it's nothing to do with sleep, darling."

"Why did I give you a key?" Too many people had access to his house. Jamie refused to move despite the chill in the air. He longingly eyed the quilt on the floor but wasn't sure he'd get to it. Dane was smaller than him, but he could wrestle cows and feral kittens, so he didn't like his chances.

"He's still not talking to me." Liam had just dropped off the face of the earth. Jamie had resorted to watching his vlog, hoping to get an update.

"Well, he certainly thinks you were a knob, sweetheart." Dane didn't mince his words.

Jamie rolled onto his back with a groan and flung his arm over his eyes. Humiliation churned in his stomach and made him feel vaguely sick. "Fucking *Paul*." It was all his fault. Jamie hadn't expected Liam to stay away. He was so sure that, when he calmed down, he'd see reason, but it had been radio silence, and now he wasn't sure Liam was ever going to speak to him again.

"Don't be such a drama queen. Have you tried going to see him? I'm not going to let you wallow like a pig in shit anymore."

Jamie sat up and glared. "I'm not wallowing. I'm hurt. I'm annoyed at myself. I said some shitty things to him that I didn't mean. And I'm worried about his rats."

"Get dressed. I'll make you breakfast, and then we'll take Speedy G for a walk." Jamie only then realised Dane's dog was sitting on the end of his bed, head cocked to one side, his little tail wagging.

"Sorry for ignoring you, Speedy." As soon as Jamie said his name, Speedy G lunged himself into his lap and wriggled on his back. Jamie laughed, tickled his belly, and leaned down so the dog could lick his face.

"Wonderful. How come I didn't get a greeting like that?" Dane crossed his arms in mock anger.

"You're not as cute," Jamie said, and Dane laughed even though they both knew it wasn't true.

Jamie absently scratched Speedy's ears and stared at Dane, wishing there was a spark between them. It would be so much easier if there were. Dane was handsome and tall, willowy but strong, he liked animals, and he liked being outdoors. They had a lot in common. It should be easy to fall in love with him, but the thought just made him feel a little sick, as though he were perving on his brother.

Dane wrinkled his nose and backed away. "Don't look at me like that."

"Like what?"

He pointed his finger accusingly at him. "Like you're undressing me and hoping that spark will fly right out of my boxers."

Jamie snorted and pushed the dog aside. "Maybe you should check for a spark in mine?" It was a joke but with a hint of seriousness to it, which was mostly born of desperation.

"Not even if you were the last man on earth, darling. Which I know you're relieved about. If I took you up on that offer, you'd go running in the opposite direction. Now. Go get dressed and meet me in the kitchen in ten minutes."

Jamie had the quickest shower on record and then threw on his clothes and padded down to the kitchen in his bare feet. There was a bowl of Frosties going soggy on the table, and Dane was leaning against the kitchen counter, drinking a cup of coffee.

"I thought you were making me breakfast?"

Dane pointed at the bowl. "Don't say I don't do anything for you."

Jamie rolled his eyes and gave a small smile. "I wouldn't call this breakfast."

"Tell that to Cereal Killer Café."

Jamie picked up the bowl and ate the milky mush. He didn't bother sitting down; they always seemed to congregate and stand in the kitchen, even if there was plenty of room to sit. "Your empathy skills suck, you know," he said with his mouth full.

"My patients don't think so."

"Your patients are mostly dogs and cats. They don't count." Jamie finished his cereal and put the bowl in the sink. "Come on. Are we going for that walk, or what?" He was not going to admit it to Dane, but he was feeling a bit more human, and he appreciated a good friend.

It was drizzling when they got to Castle Ring, and Jamie pulled his hood down over his eyes as they walked along the edges of what was once an Iron Age fort but was now a series of grassy verges and rolling hills.

Speedy G wore a small wax jacket and looked like a little old man. He ran for a tennis ball, shot down the hills, and then zoomed back up. Jamie felt he was finally coming out of his own bubble. He'd been so caught up in Liam that he'd forgotten about his friends.

"I'm getting sick of me and my problems. I don't know how to fix it right now. How are you doing? What's going on with Ben?" He bumped his shoulder against Dane's and attempted to give a smile. He'd noticed that his two friends had started to spend more time together.

Dane laughed, but it was stilted. "I don't know what you mean."

"Really?" Jamie raised an eyebrow. "You've seemed awfully cosy lately. Do you feel more for him than friendship? You do know he's not gay, right?" He was sure Dane knew that, but he didn't want him to get the wrong idea. Ben was a quiet guy and had only just started to come out of his shell.

Dane walked faster and called for Speedy, who raced back and circled his legs with a small yip. "I know that, darling, probably more than you do. Contrary to popular belief, gay and… *not*-gay men can become friends."

"True." Jamie dropped the subject because Dane gave off the vibe that he didn't want to speak about it.

"I don't want to talk about boring ol' me. We need to decide what you're going to do to apologise to Liam."

"I don't know. Paul's head on a stick, maybe?"

Dane snorted. "I think that's something you'd want more than him."

It was true. He was so angry at Paul. He wanted to throttle him, at the very least. And Jamie didn't understand him at all. He had the man he wanted—why mess with them?

The heavens opened and the drizzle turned to buckets. Despite his waterproof jacket, Jamie still got soaked down to his undies. The sky darkened, but they'd walked this path a million times before, so neither of them were concerned.

"I heard from Tommy's cousin twice removed that he and Paul have split up."

Jamie stumbled in a puddle. "What?" His feet started to get wet, but he didn't move.

"I know. Neither of them has mentioned it to me." Dane frowned. "Which is understandable, as I've not seen either of them since before the rat switcharoo."

"Son of a— I'm going around there." Things were suddenly starting to make sense. He might not be able to sort out his problems with Liam, but he could confront Paul.

Speedy G dropped the ball at his feet, and he bent down, grabbed it, and threw it with such force the dog had to zoom ahead of them to catch up with it. He pretended it was Paul's head as it bounced on the ground and Speedy caught hold of it and bit into it with sharp teeth and a shake of his head. Jamie stepped backwards out of the puddle, spun around, and walked back toward his car.

"Where are you going?" Dane called after him.

Jamie looked over his shoulder. "Where do you think? Tommy's." He was going to have it out with Paul. Dane jogged after him, calling for Speedy.

"What a fucking bastard," Jamie muttered, more to himself than to Dane. "I'll drop you off first."

"I can come with you," Dane offered, but Jamie shook his head. While he appreciated the offer, he needed to do this alone.


TOMMY LIVED in a block of apartments near the train station. It was too close to the centre of town for Jamie's liking, but even he had to admit that the apartments were nice and gave the illusion of privacy while being close to the action. They were all built in a semicircle, with a communal garden in the middle and trees around the edge. The buildings were made of cheery red brick, and all the window frames were sparkling white. Jamie parked the car and pressed the buzzer three times, waited a few seconds, and then gave it another long jab.

Finally he heard the little click and Tommy's tinny voice. "Yeah?"

"It's Jamie. Let me up."

The door opened, and Jamie jogged up the flight of stairs to Tommy's apartment. Tommy was already at the door, waiting with arms awkwardly folded, eyes guarded. They hadn't really spoken since before he'd run off with Paul.

"Where is he?" Jamie demanded, looking over Tommy's shoulder into the apartment.

"Who?"

Jamie rolled his eyes. "Stop pretending you don't know. Where the fuck is your boyfriend?"

Tommy snorted, and a tight laugh burst out of his lips that made Jamie wince. Tommy tightened his hand on the doorframe as he picked at some chipped paint. "We split up." Dane was right, then.

"What? When?" he said, pretending to be shocked.

"You better come in." Tommy stepped aside, and Jamie walked through the familiar door. It had been ages since he'd been there, and it still had an air of familiarity, though so many things had changed.

Jamie could feel Paul there, from the new cushions on the sofa to the collection of bow ties in a pile on the coffee table. There was a photo frame of them, and Paul was looking into Tommy's eyes rather than at the camera. Paul's shoes were on the rack in the hallway. His collection of commemorative fifty-pence pieces—a collection given to him by his nan when he was younger—were hanging in a wooden frame on the wall to the left of the fireplace. They'd never gotten around to putting them up at Jamie's, and in the time Paul had lived there, he'd forgotten all about them. It made something twist uncomfortably in Jamie's stomach.

If he was so much at home here, then why was he screwing with Jamie's life? Why had they split up? "Doesn't look like he's left."

Tommy dropped down into his favourite armchair, hands in his hair, and Jamie sat on the edge of the sofa, his anger fading slowly despite him trying to hold on to it.

"Yeah, well, he'll be back to collect his crap." Tommy didn't sound happy about it.

"When did all this happen?" Jamie could guess, but he wanted Tommy to admit it.

"A few weeks ago." Tommy closed his eyes as though it was too painful to talk.

"Of course it was." Just in time to mess with his life. How had Jamie not known how vindictive Paul was? They'd been together over two years.

Nervous energy had him unable to sit still, and he tapped his foot erratically while he stood in the middle of the living room. Tommy opened his eyes again and frowned at him. "He's fucking me over, and I'm not even his boyfriend anymore," Jamie said, the anger returning, flames licking at his words.

"What did he do?" Tommy didn't sound very surprised that something had happened.

"He turned up at my place, and he put one of my male rats in with Liam's females."

Tommy's shoulders relaxed, and he laughed. "Is that all?"

"Is that all? Don't you realise how dangerous that is? I'm not going to explain it to you, but I want you to keep him away from me." Tommy knew him well enough not to laugh at something like that. So what if they hadn't spoken properly for months? They'd spent years being best friends.

"Didn't you hear me? We're not together anymore," Tommy said, the laughter draining from his voice.

"I don't care. You had him last. He's your problem until some other sucker takes him on."

"Don't talk about him like that."

Jamie shook his head, a bitter smile on his lips. Couldn't Tommy see that Paul had finally gone too far? He must see something if they'd split up, so Jamie wasn't sure why he was defending him.

"Well, here I was thinking I'd be able to get my clothes in peace. No such luck," Paul said, making them both jump. Jamie twisted around to glare at him, so angry he wanted to break something, preferably Paul's face.

Despite splitting up with the boyfriend he'd left him for, Paul looked as well-groomed as ever, his trademark braces in place over a plain green T-shirt, hair perfectly coiffed. Tommy looked devastated in comparison.

Jamie's fist connected with Paul's mouth, and his knuckle caught on a tooth and split open. Paul reeled backwards, cupping a hand to his mouth in shock. Jamie's hand throbbed, and his knuckle stung, but he left his hand loose at his side, not wanting them to realise how much thumping him had hurt.

"You bastard," Paul said, voice muffled, lip swelling. Tommy stood between them. It was obvious he still cared for Paul and wanted to go to him. "Why did you hit me?" Paul said over Tommy's shoulder as though he had no clue. That just made Jamie want to thump him again.

"Why did you come to my house? Was it just to switch the rats around and fuck with me and Liam?" Another thought came to him while he was shouting, and it just wouldn't leave. "How the hell did you even know those were Liam's rats? Out of all the rats in that room, and you pick his?" It was all premeditated, but Jamie just didn't know why.

Paul gave an unhappy laugh, muffled by the hand still pressed to his sore mouth. "Come on. I've watched his videos. They're easy to spot." He stopped trying to deny knowing anything about it.

Jamie went after him again, and Tommy stepped in and pushed him back.

"Why? I don't get it," Jamie bit out, glaring at Tommy and giving him a shove because he was just so angry.

Paul moved his hand. His lip was split, and blood coated his front teeth. "Of course you don't, because you're perfect—perfect boyfriend, perfect job, perfect life. Now Tommy's given me my marching orders, you'll get your best friend back." Paul looked at Tommy, and the usual smiling mask cracked as his bottom lip started to tremble. He sucked in a breath, fingers curled so tightly into fists that his nails must be digging in. "And I'll be on my own again." His voice wobbled, and he turned it into a cough, eyes flitting around the room, not looking at either of them.

"I was perfectly fine never seeing you guys again. It's you who brought it to my doorstep. Sort your shit out and leave me the hell alone, got it?" Jamie laughed at them, and tears stung his eyes. "You don't even realise what you've done, do you?" Not only was his relationship with Liam in question, but his reputation as a breeder was on the line.

"You don't know what you've done to me either. Why couldn't you just forgive us—or at least Tommy? He's so guilt ridden that he's done nothing but push me away, just so you'll be his friend again. I don't know what to do." Paul ran his hand through his hair, undoing the perfect quiff.

"It's not like that," Tommy said to Paul.

"Isn't it? Seems that way to me. Our relationship was better when we were sneaking around." Tommy winced and looked at Jamie.

"I don't fucking care about you and your relationship. Just stay away from me and mine." If he still had a relationship.

There was so much more he had planned to say, words that could bruise and leave Paul bloodied as much as any fist could, but in that moment, Jamie realised it didn't even matter. He needed to make things right with Liam. He was all that mattered, and Jamie had forgotten about that in the big picture.

# Chapter Twenty-Eight

LIAM HAD been single most of his adult life. It shouldn't be so difficult now. Jamie was just one man. In the immortal words of Bowie, he had no power over him. His family and Selena didn't understand why he was so hurt by it all. Who cared about rats? They didn't get that it was Jamie's reaction more than what happened.

Since he first brought Mabel home, he'd been met with confusion, distaste, laughter. No one understood why he loved a rat. Rats were vermin. They certainly weren't pets. He hadn't let their words get to him because he knew how wonderful she was. From the moment she'd sat terrified in his hands, he knew she was going to be his.

Then he met Jamie, and everything changed. Finally he found someone who understood. It was amazing. Jamie had so much knowledge, and Liam got sucked into his world. But now he'd seen a side to Jamie he didn't like very much, and he didn't know how to process it.

If Jamie was still that fake rebound boyfriend, then Liam would be out there hunting for a new one, talking about it on YouTube, and lapping up the attention. But Jamie wasn't, and Liam wasn't that bloke anymore.

Even Alice could see he wasn't the same. He never would have sought her out to cry on her shoulder. She was usually a person he avoided. But she took one look at his ashen face when he turned up at her doorstep and dragged him inside—even opened a fresh packet of chocolate bourbons. He gave her a wan smile; he appreciated the gesture.

"Come on, bab. It can't be that bad," she said, and he explained what had happened.

It was obvious she truly didn't understand the rat side of things, but at least she didn't downright laugh the way Selena had. She was sweet and kind, plied him with tea and hugs, but there was no real comprehension of just how bad it was.

"I'm sure he cares more than you think, love."

Liam ran a hand through his hair and realised he'd forgotten to brush it that morning. He must look a mess. "That's part of the problem. He cares more about keeping it quiet than he does about the rats."

"He does have experience with the breeding. Maybe you should listen." She looked puzzled, but at least she was trying.

"He doesn't want any of the other breeders to find out what happened." He lowered his gaze to the table and pressed the chocolate crumbs with the pad of his finger. His heart felt bruised, and he was at a loss as to what to do.

"Relationships suck, bab. Believe me, I'm marrying your cousin. You have to compromise and talk things through, though."

Liam snorted and scowled into his tea. "*He's* not compromising at all." It was Jamie's way or no way. Why wasn't Jamie trying to see things from his point of view? He hadn't done anything wrong, yet he was being made to feel like crap.

Alice hugged him and shook her head with a smile. "You're like a teenager in his first relationship, love. Even the little things seem epic. Cry it out and then let him apologise." If only it were that simple.

"I'm going to end up a single rat father." He imagined his flat overrun, and he groaned.

"Well, love. You know what they say about kids? It takes a village."

He'd never heard that before, but he thought he understood. "Thanks, Al."

His heart was still heavy when he left Alice's, but he had someone on his side, and that made him feel a fraction better.

Jamie texted and left messages, but Liam didn't reply to any of them. He had an influx of new clients keeping him busy, plus his vlog, as well as finding out how to look after pregnant rats. He had no time to dwell or reply. Jamie needed to say sorry, not stick his foot in it further.

Lux—it really was his name, as Liam had seen on his provisional driver's licence—was a nineteen-year-old deaf student who wanted to learn with Liam because he knew fluent BSL. Liam texted him when he pulled up outside his house, and he appeared moments later. He hopped out of the driver side, settled into the passenger side, and adjusted his extra mirrors.

Lux grinned and signed a quick hello. He put on his seat belt and then twisted around to face Liam and asked, *How are you?* by curling his fingers into a loose ball, pointing his thumbs at his chest, and then bringing his hands up into a double thumbs up position.

He wouldn't want to know how Liam was really feeling, so as most English people did when someone asked them that, he automatically signed back that he was fine and added four fingers to his mouth to say *thank you.*

Initial greetings over, Liam used BSL to tell him what they were going over in that lesson and to remind him what signals he'd be using to let him know where they were going.

In the years he'd been giving lessons to the hard of hearing, Liam had it down to a fine art, using a combination of simple BSL and simple hand gestures they could see from the corner of their eye. A pointing-forward motion meant straight on, thumb to the left meant next left, thumb to the right, next right. Palm down toward the floor meant more gas, palm up toward the roof meant less gas. He had to adapt to each client, but for the most part, they worked.

Lux gave him the thumbs up sign and then concentrated on the car, turning the key, checking his mirrors again, and then finding his biting point.

He was bone tired when he finally got home that evening. He might even be exhausted enough to sleep. The last thing he needed was to see the person waiting at the entrance to his first-floor converted flat. It wasn't Jamie; he'd know his silhouette anywhere. But he recognised the willowy stance that could only belong to Dane.

"Go away." He placed his key into the lock and cursed silently when it took him a few attempts.

"Can I speak with you just for five minutes?" Dane leaned against the brick wall as he watched Liam fumble with the key.

"No." Jamie shouldn't get his friends to do his dirty work.

"At least let me check your rats. Jamie is worried, despite what you may think." He pushed the door open, and Dane shot a hand out, forcing it to stay open.

"Well, he had a funny way of showing it. Fine. You can check them. I think Gertrude and Mabel are pregnant." It was the first time he'd said it out loud to someone.

"Jamie tried to let you know that there's a medication that we can give rats if we suspect an accidental pregnancy. He's worried Maud and Gertrude are too young for it."

"That's not what he was worried about. He wanted to get rid of the evidence. He doesn't want all his fancy rat friends to know that he messed up and got some of his boarders knocked up."

"Paul was sneaky. None of us knew he was that vindictive."

Liam walked faster up the hallway and jogged up the stairs, happy when Dane cursed as he followed slightly behind.

He motioned Dane inside. "They're fine." He'd looked up the symptoms online so he'd know what to look for. He didn't need Dane or Jamie.

"Hey, girl, do you want to come out?" Dane said as he walked toward the rat cage.

Gert was the closest to the door, so he opened it, and she scrambled into his arms. Traitor.

"You're right. I'd say this one is pregnant." Dane held her up and looked at the roundness of her belly. It didn't take a genius or a vet to work that out.

She didn't want to go back in the cage, so Liam took her and let her burrow into his hoodie. Dane examined Mabel and Maud, holding them in an easy manner that showed he'd spent a lot of time around rats.

"Yep, Mabel too. I'll check the other one, just in case."

"Just my luck. Stuck as a single father," Liam muttered under his breath, wondering where he was going to put the extra cages.

Dane looked up from the rats. "You know, it doesn't have to be like that. Jamie was just freaked out about getting something wrong."

He gave a small smile. "He rarely gets much wrong, but when he does—he really does."

Liam gave a sharp laugh. "It doesn't even matter." He didn't know which way was up anymore. His heart ached, and his throat was constantly sore from swallowing unshed tears.

"You should let him explain, at least."

Liam ignored Dane's last comment. "I don't want an explanation. He said he was sorry about what happened to the rats, but he said some other really shitty things that have nothing to do with you." It wasn't easy to forgive and forget. "Thanks for checking the rats, but I think it's time for you to leave."

Of course Dane would try to plead Jamie's case. Liam went back to his front door and opened it pointedly. He was sick of feeling like this, he wanted to forget about Jamie and his friends.

Dane squeezed Liam's arm as he left. "Think about it." Liam stepped back into his flat, and Dane took that as his cue to leave.

Liam shut the door and let out a sigh of relief. Fatigue washed over him. He gave the girls a treat, went to rummage in the kitchen for his own snack, and only felt slightly pathetic when all he could find was half a jar of Nutella and a spoon.

Practically falling onto his sofa, he turned on the TV, settled on reruns of *Top Gear*, and devoured the rest of the Nutella until he started to go stir crazy and needed to leave the house before he drowned in his own tears.

He couldn't believe how low he'd fallen. Once upon a time on a Saturday night, he would be on some random date or at the clubs on the prowl. He slammed the jar on the table and quickly went to freshen up, determined to go and have a life.

He got the train into Birmingham and joined the throng of people on the street, all out to have a good time. He bypassed Broad Street, Birmingham's main party street, full of girls in tiny dresses and high heels, in favour of the village. He slipped into the first bar he came to, giving Nightingale's a wide berth.

It was one of those bars that had a small dance floor in the middle of the room and flashing lights above a sea of writhing bodies that swayed in time to the beat of the music. Liam became a contortionist as he twisted between them and sidled up to the bar. With a smile and a wink that he didn't feel, he had a drink in hand.

He was regretting leaving the house when a body bumped into him. His beer foamed up out of the bottle and down over his hand before he quickly covered the opening with his mouth and caught the rest.

"Sorry," the stranger shouted, sliding his hands up Liam's arms and roaming his gaze down his body.

"That's okay," he shouted back.

The stranger stepped forward, a mischievous half smile forming on his lips, and a sliver of excitement shot through Liam's belly. Why shouldn't he have a good time? He forced himself to stay still and smiled.

"Dance?" the man asked as he pulled Liam toward the dance floor. Liam didn't have the words to say no. He downed his bottle of San Miguel and shoved it onto a sticky table without stopping.

The stranger pressed himself against Liam and danced so close that all he could do was place his hands on his hips and hold on. It felt wrong. His hips didn't fit into the curve of his hands, and he was too short and thin. He wasn't Jamie.

He smelled of expensive aftershave and not the masculine earthy scent of a man who worked outdoors.

"You don't remember me, do you?" he shouted into Liam's bad ear. Liam turned his head and got him to repeat it. Liam frowned and leaned back to take in his features. The hair was brown, and he couldn't tell what colour the dark eyes were, but there was a familiarity about him Liam couldn't quite place.

"I'm Rowan." He could tell Liam was having difficulty hearing him, so he manoeuvred them to the edge of the dance floor, away from the speakers. "We met at the rat show."

Liam blinked, and his mouth dropped open in surprise. It took him a second to place the face, but then he remembered—the guy he'd bumped into trying to get to Jamie. He swore inwardly. Even when he was trying to forget about Jamie, it all came back to him.

"I remember." Liam gave up the pretence of dancing, but Rowan was still swaying against him, his hands hooked around Liam's neck.

What would have happened if he'd allowed himself to be sidetracked by Rowan at the rat show? Would he still be vlogging his dates, would he have fucked Rowan? He shuddered at the thought, and Rowan groaned and pressed himself closer, thinking the reaction was because of him.

Liam grabbed his arms and pulled them away from his neck. "Sorry. I can't do this." Rowan stepped into him, slipping his arms from Liam's grasp to slide them around his waist.

"Why? You're not with anyone...."

Liam gave a small, uncomfortable laugh and stepped back. "I am." He and Jamie hadn't officially broken up.

Rowan frowned, his hands freezing. "What? The rat breeder? I thought.... I mean *he* said...."

Liam was getting more confused by the second. He dragged Rowan away from the music and found a quiet corner in the small corridor between the toilets, next to a fake potted plant.

"What did you mean, '*he said*'?" Liam pressed, a niggling sense of unease slowly growing.

Rowan bit his lip and shifted nervously from foot to foot. "I watch your vlog," he admitted. It wasn't the first time he'd met people who watched his vlog, but he could tell there was more to it than that.

"And?"

"I'm the one who suggested you go to a rat show. I thought we'd meet in real life and hit it off, but you only had eyes for him." He was talking about Jamie, and Liam had to stifle his anger at the tone of his voice. The slight stalker vibe also made his skin crawl.

"How did you know I'd be here?" Liam hadn't even known that.

Rowan shrugged and looked up when some men stumbled from the toilet and swayed toward the bar. "Someone messaged me. They must have seen my comments on your videos. They said you were single again. I didn't follow you here, if that's what you mean, I just saw you here and couldn't believe my luck."

"I don't know who messaged you, but it's not true. Stay away from me, got it—online and in real life. You're about this close to becoming a stalker." He motioned an inch between his thumb and forefinger.

Liam pushed past him, needing to get out of there. He wasn't ready to forgive Jamie, but he wasn't ready to find someone else either.

"Fuck you. I tried everything to get you to like me. I suggested you go to that stupid rat show. You were meant to fall for me, not him. Then you changed your vlog for him, and I was heartbroken. I thought I'd lost my chance, and then this bloke called Paul messaged me—"

"Paul?" Liam's hand shot out, and he grabbed Rowan's arm. "His name was Paul?" Rowan shrugged out of Liam's hold and placed his hands on his hips.

"I don't know him, but he said you and the rat breeder split up."

"Fucking Paul." It had to be Jamie's ex; he didn't know another Paul. He had a serious screw loose. Liam's heart rate sped up, and he walked away, leaving Rowan shouting something after him.

He was bloody furious as he rode the last train home. It was so packed he couldn't get a seat, and the drunks were leery and not as funny as they thought they were. He fired off a text to Jamie, so mad that his ex was watching his videos purely to cause trouble.

*Tell your ex to leave me & my followers alone. I'm blocking him and reporting him.*

# Chapter Twenty-Nine

"YOU ARE a bloody fool, and if he doesn't throttle you, I certainly will," Jan said. Jamie sighed, closed his eyes, and leaned back on her sofa.

"I know. I don't know what I was thinking—I wasn't thinking." Unable to take it anymore, he'd caved and gone to see Jan and spilled the beans. "He hasn't responded to any of my messages, and then I got a random text telling me to tell Paul to leave him alone. I have no clue what that even means." He tried ringing him to ask, but Liam had gone back to radio silence.

"I would have walked out on you too. God knows what that text meant, but it can't be anything good. I never liked that man."

"He was never this much trouble until we split up."

"Not that you know of. Enough about him. What are you going to do about Liam?"

"I don't know. I freaked out, and I was selfish. He won't speak to me at all now. I asked Dane to go around and check on the rats for him. They're fine. Two are pregnant, so it could be worse. It's frustrating. I was trying to be responsible, but he wouldn't see reason. I feel like shit." His voice cracked, and Jan softened and pulled him in for a rough hug. How could he think she would judge him?

"Us rat breeders aren't perfect, you know. We all make mistakes, and this wasn't exactly your mistake, was it?"

He shook his head and relaxed into her arms. "But I was supposed to be watching them. Imagine if it was an ordinary boarder and not Liam?" They both shuddered. "Now how do I fix it when he won't talk to me?"

"I don't know, hon. But it seems to me that the damage is done, and you need to suck it up and apologise now."

"How can I do that when he won't speak to me?"

They talked a while longer, and Jamie soaked in her affection. She was like a surrogate mother and a bossy teenager all in one, and he loved her to bits. She was a great mentor and a wonderful rat breeder.

The idea came to him so suddenly he flinched. "What?" Jan said. His heart raced, and he stumbled to his feet and looked for his shoes. He needed to get out of there.

"I've got an idea. Sorry, Jan—no time to explain." He pressed a loud kiss to her cheek, making her laugh, and he finally found his shoes and almost fell as he shoved his feet into them and then ran out to his car.

As soon as he walked through the doors, he powered up his computer, went to YouTube, and managed to set up an account. That done, he typed in Liam's favourite singer. He recognised a few of the songs, but there were many other weird and obscure ones that were catchy. Deciding which one to use was more difficult than he expected. He hadn't thought he'd enjoy Phase quite so much. Finally he picked a song called "Old Memories of My New Love." It was fast and loud on the piano, and Phase practically screamed lyrics that were sweet and poignant.

He picked apart the rhythm, stripped it back piece by piece so he could build it back up and rearrange it for the uke. He played that song until his fingers ached and his callused tips became blistered.

The lyrics were easier to learn once he found them online, and he took his time singing them and turned it into a sweet love song. He wasn't a natural singer, but he could just about hold a tune, so he wouldn't sound like an *X Factor* reject.

His throat became dry, and his hands were shaking, but he finally had it down to the point where he wouldn't have to read the lyrics. He gave himself a break from the music and set up his own YouTube channel. Nerves made his breath catch, and he swallowed as he turned on his webcam and clicked Record. He sat on his office chair and wheeled backwards until he was in the middle of the room and he could see himself properly on the computer.

When he was finally ready, his throat ached with emotion, and his voice was croaky when he started to speak.

"Hi. Most of you don't know me. Some of you might know my boyfriend, though. Liam." He gave a sad smile and looked down so he didn't have to see himself on the computer. "At least I hope he's still my boyfriend. You see, I did a shitty thing." He tightened his hands on the neck of the uke as he tried to calm himself. "I was wrong. I'm sorry, Bowie. So very sorry. And…." He bit his lip—should the first time he said this be on screen? His heart thudded. If Liam didn't forgive him, he might not get to say it at all. "I love you."

# Chapter Thirty

I'm Sorry & I <3~ You
*RatPackRanger*
16K Views. 3 hours ago

Liam's ringtone woke him up. He turned over in bed, expecting to see Jamie's name pop up, and was a little shocked and then worried when it was MC Glamour. Had Rowan said something to him? He hoped not. He was still a little creeped out by it all. He flung his arm out to grab his phone but sent it sliding across the bed.

"MC? Is everything okay?" He stifled a yawn and wiped at the sleep in his eyes.

"Okay? Okay?" he screamed. Liam winced and held the phone farther away from his ear. "Don't you check social media? What kind of YouTuber are you?"

"What? Not tonight. I was sleeping," he said.

"Sometimes I think you're slow as well as half-deaf," MC sniped, but Liam didn't take offence. "Check your Twitter, check YouTube, check everything. Stop sleeping. Call me back later."

He hung up, and Liam stared at his phone with a puzzled look and finally noticed all the notifications. He even had a text from Abigail, telling him to check YouTube. Had Rowan done something?

His Twitter handle, LofaRider, had hundreds of notifications and retweets, but he had no clue what they were talking about. He scrolled through the clutter of messages and found a new follower—RatPackRanger. His heart plummeted. It was easy to guess who that was. Despite knowing he should ignore it and block him, Liam couldn't stop his interest, not with all the other people tagging him in everything and using #ratpackranger.

Without thinking too deeply, he clicked on the very first tweet Jamie had tagged him in. It simply said, *I'm sorry, give me a second chance,* and then gave a link to YouTube. He couldn't not follow it through, so he hit the link and opened a shoddily made video that made him let out a shaky laugh despite wanting to stay strong.

It was poorly lit, the desk lamps bleached out the colour a little, and it was obviously videoed on Jamie's computer. He was sitting on his office chair with his ukulele balanced on his lap.

"Hi. Most of you don't know me. Some of you might know my boyfriend, though. Liam. At least I hope he's still my boyfriend. You see, I did a shitty thing. I was wrong. I'm sorry, Bowie. So very sorry. And…."

Jamie played dirty; he knew Liam couldn't resist him when he called him Bowie. His legs started to tremble, and he felt stupid because of it.

"I love you."

The air disappeared from Liam's lungs, and he gave a wheezing gasp. Sweat beaded on his forehead, and he peered closer at the phone, wishing Jamie were really in front of him. Those three words changed everything.

"For those who don't know anything about me—I'm a fancy rat breeder. I met Liam at a pet rat show when he was filming a video for his vlog." He gave the sweetest smile. "He respected my privacy because he knew I was uncomfortable being on film, but I did something stupid. I was looking after his rats, and one of my bucks ended up in the same cage. I was so scared what the other rat breeders would say that I didn't stop to think about him. I also said some shitty things about his vlog and his business. I didn't mean it, Bowie. I just lashed out and I knew that would hurt you. I'm so sorry." He bit his lips, hand clutching the neck of the uke.

"I'm not concerned, worried, or scared anymore—not about that. I'm petrified you'll leave me, though." He gave a grimace and licked his lips "I just wanted to say that I love you. And I'm sorry."

He rotated his shoulders in that adorably awkward way he had when he knew people were watching him. Liam's heart swelled. Loving Jamie always came so easily. It was one of the reasons this hurt so much. Liam half sobbed, half laughed, and his eyes burned with tears.

"I thought I'd play you a song, Bowie." The nickname turned his insides to mush, and his heart swelled. He'd missed hearing it.

There was more? He expected a David Bowie song, but when the first chords of Phase's "Old Memories of My New Love" started, Liam forgot about everything but watching him and taking in every small detail.

"*How is it that I know you so well when we've only just met? Years of memories not shared yet,*" Jamie sang. The lyrics sounded so sweet coming from his lips. When Phase sung that song, it was loud and harsh, but Jamie had turned it into the love song it was always meant to be.

His fingers were slightly hesitant on the strings at first, but as soon as he got into the song, it was as though he was transported to the stage.

Tears burned tracks down Liam's cheeks as he listened.

"*Your eyes, they remind me of the first time I loved you—years ago—how can it be we've only just met. Do you sneak into my dreams? Do you? Do you?*"

Now that he was hearing Jamie's version of the song, he could barely remember the original. He shivered, goosebumps covering his arms, and the hairs on his arms stood on end. The arrangement was beautiful, changed perfectly so the song became their song, the lyrics about their life.

Jamie looked pale on the other side of the screen. Even with bags under his eyes, he was beautiful. Liam's body ached just to be near him. He wanted to press his face into Jamie's curly hair, smell his spicy shampoo, and feel his body wrapped around his.

Tears were still burning down his cheeks and settling into the corners of his mouth until he could taste salt. He let out a shaky laugh and wiped his eyes with the back of his hand. Out of everything Jamie could have done, Liam hadn't expected this.

"*Like well-worn memories, you make me feel so much more.*"

Liam's whole body shivered. He pulled the quilt over his bare shoulders and held the phone close to his face. There was something so incredibly intimate about knowing Jamie was singing in front of the whole world, entirely for him.

Jamie's voice and each pluck of the strings warmed Liam's heart. Jamie had outed his mistake to the entire world.

He finished singing and licked his lips. "I really do love you." Then he got up and pressed Stop, cutting off the image.

There were already hundreds of comments on his video, most of them telling Liam to forgive him. There was no question. He didn't bother trying to write something back. Jamie had said sorry in a way he knew Liam would appreciate, and he needed to do the same. Scrambling out of bed, he pulled on his dirty jeans and the *L of a Ride* T-shirt he'd worn the night before. He needed to get to Jamie as soon as possible.

He didn't use his key when he got to Jamie's. He just knocked his knuckles against the wood. Jamie yanked open the door, eyes widening and shoulders relaxing. "Thank God," he said. His hair stuck out in all directions, his mouth was strained, and he looked like he'd lost weight.

"You definitely know how to apologise." Liam half smiled, unsure what to say now he was there.

"I'm so fucking sorry." Jamie's voice cracked, and Liam folded him into his arms and stroked his hair, soaking up the feel of him.

He shuddered as their bodies pressed together again. He'd been cold inside for weeks, but just the press of Jamie's warm, hard body against his made him feel alive.

Jamie kept mumbling, "Sorry, so sorry," into his neck, and Liam pressed featherlight kisses to the side of his face.

"It's okay. I'm sorry too."

Jamie leaned back, and his eyes were bright. His lips trembled, and Liam couldn't stand to see him cry, so he kissed him instead. It was light at first but deepened quickly. Jamie tasted of salty tears and toothpaste.

Liam pulled back with a half smile. "You said something else in that video." He couldn't forget the heartfelt "I love you." It was the first time anyone had ever said that to him, and it was the first time he'd felt it for someone else.

Jamie's eyes widened, and he licked his lips. "I love you." His voice was shaky, full of emotion, and Liam felt his throat swell with something warm and soft that filled him up from head to toe.

"I love you too." He pulled him back into his arms and held tight. How had he gone so long without this?

They kissed again, and Jamie backed into the house. Liam fumbled behind himself to shut the door. When he heard it click, he followed Jamie upstairs, hand in hand.

"I know we have things to talk about. I have so much to apologise for, but I just need to feel you against me for a while. Is that okay?" They ended up wrapped in the duvet, Stark purring next to them.

"You're the last person I ever want to hurt." They talked and cleared the air, and Liam told Jamie about Rowan and Paul's part in it. They agreed he was never allowed in Jamie's house again, and they had the right to ignore him if they saw him out.

"I told him to fuck off—no more keeping the peace, no more being nice. I can't believe he trolled your channel and messaged that guy."

"It's a tad stalkerish," Liam said in total agreement.

"There's seriously something wrong with him. *He* split up with *me*."

"I remember." Liam smiled and pressed a kiss to Jamie's forehead. That had been a good day for him.

"I couldn't get rid of you." He didn't sound unhappy about that. "How are the girls, by the way?" He was cautious asking, but Liam's anger and hurt had disappeared with the first "I love you."

"Dane probably told you that Mabel and Gertrude are expecting?" Jamie nodded and bit his bottom lip. Liam distracted him with a kiss. "They're doing great, though. Better than me. I'm petrified."

"Don't be. I'll help."

Liam tightened his arm around him. "Good, because I don't know what I'm doing."

Exhaustion finally caught up with them, and their conversations got slower and further apart until they finally drifted off.


IT WAS dark when he woke with a start, terror choking him, making his limbs tense. He let out a breath and sank back into the mattress when he saw Jamie beside him.

Jamie whimpered and stretched, blinked his eyes slowly, and smiled when he saw him. "Hey, Bowie."

Liam shuddered, and his cock stirred at Jamie's gravelly sleep-filled voice. He moved his hands under the blanket and fiddled with the hem of Jamie's T-shirt as he waited for permission. Jamie's eyes darkened, and he pushed the duvet down. Liam pulled the plain green T-shirt over Jamie's head and slung it across the room.

He'd lost a little weight, but not enough to do much damage to his beautifully toned abs and rock-hard chest. His Superman pyjama bottoms rode low, and with featherlight touches, Liam pressed fingers to the sharp angles of his hip bones, loving the hitch in Jamie's breath as he did so.

"I missed this, missed how you're ticklish, missed how your breath tickles my cheek when I touch you." He kept his words light as he memorised the hard lines of Jamie's body with his fingertips.

Desire curled in his belly like smoke. It was hard to breathe, his vision blacking out around the edges as he tried to suck oxygen into his lungs.

Jamie was everything he wanted in a man and more. He was real, honed from years of working outside rather than years dabbling in a gym. He had a broad chest and a tapered waist with just a hint of a six-pack. Liam placed his hand against the swirl of hair under his belly button, and the coarse hair brushed his palm and made him shiver.

The house was silent. Only their gasps and groans filled the air. Jamie's hands were clenched into fists at his side as though he were trying his hardest not to interrupt Liam's exploration. He appreciated the sentiment. Leaning over to lick the tan line around his neck, groaning as the taste of salt burst across his tongue, he moved farther down and nibbled his way to one of Jamie's nipples. He blew on it, making it tighten, and Jamie sucked in a breath and held it in as Liam scraped his nail along the other. Jamie bucked his hips and tangled his hands in Liam's hair.

"You okay?" Liam's voice was all gravel and heat as he spoke around the small nub still in his mouth.

Jamie licked his lips, his breath coming in small pants. "Do not stop."

Liam smiled, his heart warming, He swirled his tongue around the tight bud and looked up from beneath his lashes. "I won't." He couldn't if he wanted to. He needed Jamie more than he needed air.

They undressed each other without getting out of bed. Awkward pushes of fabric and tangled clothes around limbs were followed by breathless laughter. The room was stifling hot. Sweat dripped down his forehead, and Jamie leaned over and licked the droplet away.

It would have been quicker to stand, but Liam didn't want to leave the safe cocoon of blankets. As soon as they were freed from their clothes, they moved together as though they'd never been apart. Their cocks lined up as they faced each other.

Each small touch was like touching a live wire, and Liam's heart pounded with the intensity of it. He sucked in air, and it fed the fire. Each nerve ending crackled. Jamie reached between them, circled their cocks with his fingers, and pressed them together.

His eyes rolled at the sensation, and he lost the ability of speech. All he could make were grunts, whimpers, and groans. They lay face-to-face, legs sliding together as Jamie tightened his hands around them.

This was what making love was, Liam realised with clarity. Sex with Jamie was always more than just sex, even the very first time, when he tried to keep it impersonal. But what he felt right then was unexplainable.

His toes curled, and he shuddered as he tried to slow his heart rate so his chest didn't explode. He mashed his chest against Jamie's and slipped a hand over the curve of his hip. Then he slid it around to the curve of his ass and pulled their groins closer, trapping Jamie's hand between them.

Their mouths clashed, all tongue and teeth full of want and relief, but most of all, love... and it wasn't enough. Jamie smiled into the kiss, angled his head sideways, and widened his mouth to give Liam what he wanted. He tasted sweet—a touch of toothpaste and caramel coffee.

His ears roared, and a crackling noise sounded in his deaf ear that made him dizzy. Vertigo made his stomach whoosh as though they were on a roller coaster. When Jamie moved his hand against his stomach, grasping his straining erection with the callused pads of his fingers, pressing their dicks together, Liam cried out, unable to keep the sound inside. Jamie swallowed the noise and tightened his grip on them, dragging his rough fingers against the sensitive skin of Liam's erection.

Without much thought, Liam rolled them over in a tangle of limbs until Jamie lay sprawled beneath him. He laughed, breaking their kiss, and rubbed one slightly furred thigh against Liam's hip.

"You're crazy." Jamie shook his head, his curls bouncing softly. Liam caught an errant lock in his hand, pulled it straight, and watched it bounce back when he let go.

Liam kissed the smile on his lips with small biting nips that left them swollen and wet. "Remember how we first met?" Jamie asked. Of course he did. A car park in Digbeth, gravel at his back and a tangle of limbs? "Did you realise when we met that we would end up here?"

"I wanted you from the moment my head hit the gravel and you kneed me in the balls," Liam said.

Jamie laughed and slapped his arm. "I did not."

"Close enough." Liam trailed his hand down Jamie's side. "What's funny is, and what I didn't realise at the time, was that small knee nudge from you was more explosive than the blowjob I got in the escape room."

"You sweet talker, you. I will definitely knee you more often." Jamie winked and slid a leg beneath Liam's and rubbed his ball with his knee.

"Then I saw you at the rat show, and I was so happy that you were there."

"I wasn't happy at the time, but I'm definitely happy you were there now." Jamie captured his lips with his.

They kissed again, and Liam ran his hand down Jamie's side, skimmed the curve of his hip, and then hiked his leg up and over Liam's thigh. Their cocks slid against each other, and fireworks exploded behind his eyes.

"Shit," Jamie said, his words shaky. He blinked up at Liam, eyes roaming over his face. Liam didn't know what he could see, but his expression was serious. "Your eyes...." Jamie ran a hesitant finger over his forehead and touched the corner of his eye with his thumb.

Liam felt raw, exposed—emotions he hadn't felt for anyone else bubbling to the surface. His lips trembled under Jamie's gaze, and he had to look away before he did anything stupid.

Jamie reached for the condom and lube on the bedside table and handed them to him. Liam took them with shaking hands and stared at them. He licked his lips and looked back into Jamie's eyes.

"Do you?" He held the condom up, unable to finish the sentence.

"Have you?" It looked like Jamie couldn't finish one either.

He shook his head. Of course he hadn't been with anyone else. "No."

They'd taken the test and both come back clean, but it was never the right time. Now it was. Jamie cupped his hand over Liam's and then slowly took the condom from his fingers and chucked it across the room.

Liam groaned, his whole body shuddering at the thought of sinking into Jamie with nothing surrounding him. He poured lube onto his shaking fingers and reached for Jamie, bypassing his cock. He massaged his balls and then slowly trailed below and circled his hole.

Jamie whined, eyes rolling back into his head, and dug his heels into the bed as he pushed his hips upwards to give him more room. Liam was gentler than he ever remembered being as he loosened Jamie with his fingers until he was cursing with need and urging Liam to do more.

Liam coated himself and bit his lip at the sensation of his hand. He guided himself with one hand, pushing against Jamie's small ring of muscle, and slowly sank into him. He'd never done this bare before, and it was so much more than he thought it would be. He felt the tight muscle as he pushed through, felt every clench as Jamie squeezed around him and every vibration from every moan or grunt he made.

Jamie's nails bit into his shoulders, and his eyes were wide. "Oh my fucking God." Was it as intense for him? Liam slowly pulled out and thrust back in, Jamie's cries urging him on.

Jamie dug his heels into the small of Liam's back and raked his nails across Liam's shoulders. Liam's body trembled, unable to keep upright, and he fell against Jamie, his weight heavy and his thrusts erratic as their lips claimed each other.

Liam's throat swelled with so much emotion, and his eyes burned with tears. It was stupid; he shouldn't cry because of this. He gave a strangled grunt and ripped his lips from Jamie's to bite at the tender skin of his neck.

He set a brutal pace, slamming into Jamie as hard and as far as he could. Jamie tightened around his cock with the most intimate of caresses, so gentle and then fast and urgent.

Rhythm and expertise disappeared and pure instinct took over. Liam gave a breathless scream and pushed Jamie back into the bed, thrusting into him.

Knowing he was bare inside, Jamie spurred him on. He couldn't be gentle, but luckily Jamie wasn't expecting him to be. Jamie gave as good as he got, and when Liam thought he couldn't take much more, he came mere seconds after Jamie coated their stomachs. Liam collapsed on top of Jamie their chests heaving, skin sweaty, in a tangle of limbs. It was his favourite place to be.

It was as if they were always destined for this. It took a long time for Liam's heart to go back to normal, and hearing Jamie's laugh made him open one eye to stare at him.

Jamie's laugh made Liam's cock twitch with sensory overload as it slipped from Jamie's body.

"You really are the perfect rebound." Jamie tightened his arms around him, and he kissed the side of Liam's head. "I really love you."

"And you're my perfect fake boyfriend. Hey, maybe we could get married at Zombie Brum City." He was sure they'd lift his ban for a wedding.

Jamie burst out laughing. "You asking me to marry you, Bowie?"

Liam nuzzled into him with a smile. "Maybe one day."

He snorted and threw a leg over Liam's hip. "Maybe we can go on our stag do there."

# Chapter Thirty-One

IT HAD been weeks since they'd gotten back together, and their relationship was better than ever. Liam had utterly and completely won over Jamie's mom, Jan adored him, and blessedly, they hadn't seen Paul or Tommy.

Jamie was nestled in their bed, curled around Liam's pillow when Liam tried to wake him up. He didn't want to open his eyes or get out of bed. He was warm and comfy. "Come back to bed," he mumbled without opening his eyes.

"It's time," Liam said.

"Sleeping." He screwed his eyes shut and pulled the duvet over his head.

"It's time, Mr Grumpy," Liam teased. "It's *time*." He pulled the duvet away.

"Wha?" Didn't Liam know he needed sleep by now? And lots of it.

"Gert is having her babies."

"What?" Fully awake now, Jamie shoved the covers down the rest of the way, sat up, and rubbed the heel of his hand into his eyes. "Really?"

Gert and Mabel were due any time now. He gave him a large smile, slipped out of bed and into a pair of boxer shorts, and they padded barefoot to the small box room where they'd set up small cages for the expectant mothers.

The box room now had more cages just waiting for Gert and Mabel's babies. Liam's newly received silver YouTube plaque had pride of place on the wall above them. Jamie's rendition of "Old Memories of my New Love" had catapulted Liam's channel to the heights it now was. His own channel had gotten some subscriptions, even though he hadn't posted anything since. Liam did try to persuade him to start a ratty channel, but he wasn't sure if he was brave enough.

He grinned at Liam, relieved that everything looked good. They watched a little longer, and when Jamie was sure Gert wasn't in any danger, he motioned for Liam to leave the room.

"We're going to be rat fathers. I think I'm going to faint. How can you be so calm?" Liam's eyes were wide with panic, and he had a death grip on Jamie's hand.

"This isn't my first rodeo," he drawled. "Come on, let's have breakfast. We'll check on them later."

They went downstairs to make coffee, and Liam paced back and forth. "Do I need to boil water and fetch towels?"

Jamie laughed and hugged him, effectively stopping the pacing. "Only if they were human babies in Victorian times. She's doing fine."

"But these aren't your fancy pedigree rats. Shouldn't we be in there?"

Jamie tightened his grip on him and ruffled his blond hair. "They have childbearing hips," he joked. "Remember, you're the one who told me that Maud and Gert's mom did fine. Mabel's too. They're healthy, and we had Dane check them just a few days ago."

Liam snorted. "Childbearing hips? Your mom said the exact same thing to Ellen when we went around for dinner." Jamie smiled. His mom, dad, and sister loved Liam as much as Jamie did. He didn't even get embarrassed by her like he used to, and they'd become much closer because of Liam.

He and Liam sat in the kitchen, hands cupping steaming mugs of coffee in comfortable silence. They both flinched when the letterbox clacked, followed shortly by the drop of letters on the doormat.

Jamie went to retrieve the mail, flipped through them, and handed one to Liam. It was addressed to both of them using their full names, which was strange and a bit formal.

"Wonder what this is?" Liam ripped it open and pulled out the cream card with gold edging.

*Mr Liam Donnelly and Mr James Hewett.*
*Miss Alison Thorn and Mr Frank Hamilton*
*request the pleasure of your company at their marriage*

A slow smile spread across Liam's face, and he glanced up at Jamie, love shining in his eyes. He knew he'd get that bloody plus-one.

ANDI LEE lives in the UK, close enough to Birmingham city to be considered a 'Brummie', but far enough away to enjoy the Staffordshire countryside. She enjoys writing in many different genres as long as they contain a large dose of cute guys falling in love. She's a sucker for a happy ending.

When she's not writing, she enjoys making junk journals, and also jewellery out of polymer clay and resin. She has kept pet rats on and off for twenty years and fell in love with her first ferret when she found him on her way to work one day. She's kept them ever since.

(And she apparently has an obsession with Vans—the shoes not the vehicles!)

You can find her at www.andileewrites.com
Twitter: @andileewrites

FOR **MORE**
OF THE
**BEST**
**GAY**
ROMANCE

**REAMSPINNER**
PRESS
dreamspinnerpress.com

49407524R00111

Made in the USA
Lexington, KY
22 August 2019